The Gothic Twilight

BY THE SAME AUTHOR

Fear & Philosophy (fiction)
Crisis of Representation (fiction)
The Flood (visual writing)
Undeserved Reputations (visual writing)
Things (visual writing)
Invading Reagan (visual writing)
tales (fiction)
ADVANCINGreceding (visual writing)
Corona 2500 (visual writing)
Open Form & the Feminine Imagination (non-fiction)
Until It Changes (visual writing)
Poems (poetry)
Edges (poetry)

The
GOTHIC
Twilight

STEPHEN-PAUL MARTIN

Santa Maria:Asylum Arts:1992

Acknowledgements

Grateful acknowledgement is made to the editors of *Another Chicago Magazine, Avec, Fiction International, Flower Thief* and *Heaven Bone*, in which some of these stories first appeared. "Double Bed" and "The French Revolution" first appeared as a phamphlet, *Crisis of Representation*, published by Standing Stones Press.

Copyright © 1992 by Stephen-Paul Martin
All rights reserved.
Printed in the United States of America

ISBN 1-878580-45-0
Library of Congress Catalogue No. 92-70668

Cover photocollage and book design by Greg Boyd.

Notice:
The stories in *The Gothic Twilight* are works of fiction. Statements made about living human beings are not intended to be taken literally.

Asylum Arts Publishing
P. O. Box 6203
Santa Maria, CA 93456

Contents

PART ONE

Talking Disorders	9
Nailclippers	13
Shakespeare's Head	16
Double Bed	22
National Disaster	27
Fake Murders	30
The King of Noise	34
The French Revolution	38
Operation Welcome Home	43
The Gothic Twilight	47

PART TWO

New World Order	55

THE
GOTHIC
TWILIGHT

TALKING DISORDERS

She was just about to say that U.S. foreign policy is total bullshit, complete hypocrisy, or at best an exercise in self-deception, that no matter what U.S. leaders claim they're doing, their main concern is serving the needs of the nation's big corporations, producing new bacterial forms of aggression, spending billions every day on secrecy and repression, all at the expense of ninety percent of the population, the so-called common people, most of whom are kept in check by TV sets and movie screens, advertising billboards, VCRs and football scores, a state of induced passivity, dependence on the charm of representations, entertainments, making it highly unlikely that any substantial number of people, organizing nationwide with diligence and intelligence, will have the desire to mount a significant oppositional movement, settling instead for seminars of indifference, for a goldfish bowl in a vacant lot in Cleveland, for neighbors getting drunk and throwing furniture out the window, for a course in how to levitate close friends at cocktail parties.

She was just about to say all this and more, much more. But Pete cut her off with a brusque dependent clause and then a huge main clause. When Pete began talking, there was no stopping him. He had what she called a talking disorder, a supremely annoying condition that seemed to be spreading all over the nation, a condition in which a person talks non-stop, has no interest in what people might say in response, and in any case gives them no chance to respond, talking loudly and firmly over anything they might say, and on those rare occasions that a person like Pete might pause, he would have no response to, and seemingly no awareness of, anything that might be said before he began once again, launching a fresh dependent clause or maybe a massive main clause.

Had it just been Pete who spoke this way, it would have been bad enough. But she knew so many people who talked incessantly, people she often tried to avoid, but couldn't, since most were close friends, immediate relatives, public servants, or people she worked with. So she had to content herself with wondering why they were so incessant. Had they been brought up in households where people typically spoke in extended monologues, or were they desperate to control verbal interactions, or were they only interested in the sound of their own voices, or were they so out of touch that they really thought some kind of two-way interchange was occurring, or were they symptoms of mass communication, its one-way modes of presentation that left no space for response, or were they drifting down a turbulent river with a boat full of beer and a radio blasting big-hit songs from the fifties, or were they planning to go to the zoo at night and wake all the animals, or were they convinced that in the sub-atomic realm time can move in either direction, or were they trapped between the illusion of community and the community of illusion? She couldn't be sure.

But she also couldn't say anything. Pete was talking on and on, clearly amused by everything he said, firmly convinced that she was too, gesturing vividly in the dark bar they were sitting in, or rather, gesturing vividly in what might well have been a dark bar at a certain point in the not-too-distant past, but now had become a cardboard imitation, a picture torn from *Time* magazine or *Newsweek*, outside of which the landscape seemed to be made of huge tomatoes, heaped up against the windows, backdropped by the amplified sound of obscene heavy breathing, and the sound of jets breaking the sound barrier made her think of rats in a medieval dungeon, or snakes eternally sleeping in the sun in southern Utah, or sneakers hung by shoestrings from a streetlight in Toledo, or a lightshow making someone's really bad acid trip get better.

He'd been talking for maybe ten minutes now, and slowly the setting seemed to be transforming itself, and she thought she was in her own home, and the subject had seemed to change with each new sentence at first, but began to speed up, changing now with each new phrase or word, constantly moving off in different directions, all of which were unforeseen but none of which held her attention, or even seemed designed to, but appeared instead to be moving in response to internal dynamics, to changes in the shape of each word and each thing it referred to, or appeared to refer to, or to changes in atmospheric pressure, or to broken speedometers, or thirteen wild white horses near the cliffs of Tierra Del Fuego, a necktie catching fire at a Houston seance, a bad production of *Hamlet* made even worse by a front-row suicide, a frog in a mansion caving in thirty-three miles north of Nashville. She wanted to stop him and say that she felt his pattern of talking was really offensive, a disguised form of nonspecific hostility or aggression, but she knew Pete got offended when people were critical, that he tended to talk even more when he felt defensive, that he really meant no harm and was in some ways a wonderful person, that his undershirt was far too small, that his curly hair was symbolic, that the line of poplars near the place of her birth had been destroyed, that nature has no ultimate unified form, that the Gulf Stream soon would change its course and Europe would soon be frozen, that a black wet bird flies best at night, that bowling and miniature golf were slowly losing their widespread public appeal, that language is both the product and the instrument of speech.

She tried to do things to subtly give Pete a hint that he'd better stop talking, like looking at her watch and creasing her brow, or clearing her throat and looking out the window, or tapping her foot and creating a beat that differed from Pete's speech rhythms, or taking books off the shelf and dusting them off and turning their pages, slamming them shut and looking up with a gleam in her eye and a big mean smile, or calling her Saint Bernhard who came in barking and bursting with energy, or claiming she wanted to catch the president's bullshit speech on the six o'clock news, or insisting that language has nothing to do with radical formalizations, despite the clever theories that structural thinkers use to describe it, or sticking a pencil down her throat as a way to seem bulimic, or pounding pillows murmuring her parents' names, then Pete's name.

But nothing worked. Pete's words pushed and pulled, peaked and plummeted, pissed all over the parlor, plunging past her puerile protest. And each word made the setting change ever so slightly, as if his head had suddenly become much larger, filled with doors that opened and closed and people that weren't going in or out, but apparently wanted to seem as if they were, as if she and Pete were back in a dark city bar, and all her frustration began turning in on itself. She accused herself of being too passive, too passive-aggressive, or too self-absorbed to enjoy another's eloquence, or jealous that she herself didn't have the nerve to just talk about anything, or morbidly in love with silence, or half in love with easeful death, knowing well that what she really wanted was a change of pace, indeed a change of place, a chance to be doing something somewhere else, like watching a big tornado from a haunted house near Tulsa, or managing a trampoline repair shop, or waking at four a.m. with a craving for beer and buttered popcorn, or selling vaseline door-to-door in Tacoma.

The clock struck twelve and Pete got up quickly, left without a word, just as she was about to cut him off with a brusque dependent clause. Another man who said his name was Pete came in, began talking, starting with an independent clause that had no subject, none whatsoever, remarkable in its precise avoidance of meaning, in its clear suggestion that if indeed there's a highway leading to the known world, it's not in good shape at all; it needs repairs, extensive repairs that funds aren't available for, and won't be anytime soon. As Pete went on and on she tried to look past him, but what she saw behind his head in the dark bar window had no depth; it was just a big photograph, a black and white city skyline ripped half-way from the top and repaired with tape. And the obscene heavy breathing seemed to move closer.

NAILCLIPPERS

Karl was crossing the street on a day when everyone seemed to be laughing. He noticed that one of his fingernails was too long, so he reached into his pocket and got out his nailclippers. Just as he began clipping his nails, a huge guy beside him dressed in a fake general's uniform scowled and growled, told him he thought it was disgusting that Karl was clipping his nails in public.

Karl thought he wanted to punch the guy in the face, or kick the guy's balls off, but the guy was pretty big, and besides, the day was like beer getting spilled on someone's new white sofa, and there was a woman standing on the other side of the street who seemed to be thinking that space can be replaced by digital codes and glowing screens, a baby carriage beside her facing north and filled with bananas, a newspaper blowing down the street past three doorways leading up to rooms where guys were typing erotic novels, three guys typing out four books a week, as if to say that the central point of any scientific explanation is the description of an explanatory mechanism, or the explanation of a descriptive mechanism, producing under the best of conditions a day so filled with sunlight that no one can see their own feet, so Karl sort of chuckled and tried to pretend that the guy hadn't said anything, or at least not to him, but the guy kept staring at him, made a kind of disgusted noise with his mouth, and again Karl felt anger building up, the kind of rage that leads to serial murders, an obvious indication that Karl had never learned to get his anger out properly, had never learned to calmly but firmly say that he didn't like the way someone was treating him, had never learned that anger and violence aren't the same thing, that the unconscious fills with murderous intentions if feelings aren't expressed in appropriate ways, even if the unconscious turns out to be a mere concept, a mere name, a theoretical sweet-nothing, a place on a map that maps out nothing, like a dead fish in a huge abandoned parking lot near Pittsburgh, where young boys practice impossible contortions with a white frisbee, hoping that some day they can find jobs that pay pretty well and don't involve much paper work, unaware that they're trapped in a manufactured system of economic instabilities, convinced that the dualistic model of human awareness, a mapping device that leads to the fear of talking, is clearly moving into its final but deadly supernova stage, an assumption that Karl now turned away from, staring at his feet, wondering just how much of his manhood he could sacrifice in the name of acting civilized, as the big guy turned to his wife and said something Karl couldn't quite hear, but when she snickered Karl knew that the guy had said something nasty about him, and this got Karl even more pissed off, because word was spreading, soon everyone would know, they would all be disgusted, they would know that he had no place on the street, no place in a world where people had agreed to look normal, even if they weren't, even if the very notion of being normal had long ago been dismissed, exposed as a tool of social control, a buzz word that allowed stupid people to feel secure and indulge in blithe fantasies about human progress, paging through back issues of *National Geographic* in waiting rooms with muzak, waiting for novocaine or thorazine or AZT or more magazines, while through the nice clean windows a thousand fenders flashed in the sunlight, and a thousand radios hacked up the afternoon with gum jingles, airline jingles, health club jingles, political platitudes, bad jokes, contrived personalities, carefully doctored news presentations, a multitude of inanely urgent voices, and less and less intelligence to hear them with, as if to say that culture organizes itself by energizing differences, a curious mixture of big science and Hollywood fantasies, many of which had already begun to function as biochemical organisms, snarling over bleak postmodern skylines, the same ones that Karl tried at times to read articles on, turning the dreary pages of academic journals, pages that were no help to Karl standing there on the street, filling up with an anger so extreme there was no way to measure it, an anger so out of proportion to what was really happening that only a madman could even begin to unravel it, and the woman beside the big guy looked at Karl with a mixture of sympathy and contempt, but Karl could only see the contempt, or rather, he interpreted the sympathy as resignation, or perhaps

NAIL CLIPPERS

disgust, and a dog on the corner was leaning back on its haunches barking at thunderclouds, as if to say that what happens to a biochemical system depends on how that system is made, determined by its components and the relations between the components, like someone getting sick of a crossword puzzle, or the CIA deciding to murder a president, or background noise in a fictive love scene, or thoroughly subjective definitions of obscenity, or fingernails on a blackboard, or the sucked-out feeling that spread through Karl's belly toward his balls, cold then hot then cold, as he tried to master his anger, tried to pretend that nothing was happening, nothing you could make a movie out of anyway, but the traffic-light wouldn't change and Karl had to keep standing there, right beside two people he wanted to kill, and they both started laughing, not loudly or even visibly but laughing nonetheless, he could sense it behind their vaguely serious faces, and it wouldn't stop, couldn't stop, could only grow into fifteen bags of potato chips at a wedding, or broken glass on the floors of South Bronx tenements, or cave paintings destroyed by nuclear testing, or film reviews getting used as packing paper. And the big guy smiled and said: You know, it's none of my business, I'm sorry I said anything to you, it's perfectly OK if you clip your nails waiting for the light to change, if more people did it the world would be a better place to live, I'd probably do it myself if I weren't so inhibited, but that's what it's all about isn't it, inhibitions becoming prohibitions, so please accept my apologies, on behalf of everyone who's ever caused you any pain, it's all our fault, we've been wrong from the start.

But Karl knew that he couldn't accept the apology. There was too much noise. The world was too content with its own pathologies. And besides, the light was already green. He was already crossing into the future, where nothing anyone said was said in time to prevent what followed, and time was a really strange pill he'd already swallowed.

SHAKESPEARE'S HEAD

He was trapped in what could only be described as an all-encompassing change, a transformation too vast for comprehension. He might have said that the struggle between tradition and innovation, the principle of social change in all historical cultures, can only occur if innovation prevails. Yet cultural innovation is carried on by historical process, a movement which, when it starts to become aware of its own totality, tends to supersede those presuppositions that comprise it, moving to subsume all sociocultural transformation.

It's in this play of tensions that individuals form identities, which might be described as relatively autonomous totalities, zones of organization taking shape as a pattern of voices, some of which are known and some of which speak from the cultural matrix, the total historical movement they comprise and are comprised by. He knew that such formations are often accompanied by stress, temporal dislocations making the present seem retroactive. The words taking shape to inform his perceptions might have had little to do with what he was looking at, might have been parts of a past that never was, a past that took the place of the past and made it seem to move backwards. The voice that tried to get his attention might very well have been Shakespeare's. But in fact he was too far gone to care, his head was filled with fever, and the sharp November wind blew against his teeth, against his throat, blew his hair back off his face, made his hair stand up and then tore it off, it blew his nose off, drove his teeth back down his throat and finally ripped his head off, sending it bouncing down the street—until it came to rest in a baby carriage near a phone booth. His hands reached up to find his face, groped in the space where his head once was, weaving very slowly down the cracked and filthy sidewalk, stumbling around the corner just as Jill stepped out on the street.

Jill wasn't sure if she'd seen what she saw—a man without his head—but when she saw the blood-smeared face in the carriage looking stunned and stoned, she knew that losing one's head might well be more than a figure of speech, and a gap took shape in her mind instead of a thought or a clear perception. The bloody face made no conscious impression, and she went down the street undisturbed, stepped into a phone booth, called her boss and quit her job, felt clean as a newborn child, stepped into a bar near Astor Place, looking for men to talk to.

Jack stumbled in thirty-eight seconds later, sat at the bar beside her, began reading *The Killer Inside Me*.

Jill said: I just finished reading that last week! Isn't it great?

Jack said: Yeah, it's really great. And he bought her three Dos Equis.

Soon they were back in his bedroom getting to know each other in bed, but suddenly Jill turned red, held her head, remembered the face in the carriage.

O God, she said, You're not going to believe what I saw this afternoon! I saw this guy with no head walking down the street, and then I saw what must have been his head in a baby carriage.

Jack was pissed at the interruption. He said: How do you know that the head belonged on the body? It might have just been a coincidence! He jumped up out of bed and lit a cigar, went to his desk and stared out the window. Why did every woman he met have deep emotional problems? Why were they always morbidly obsessed with physical suffering? And why had cultural innovation become yet another commodity? Why had human struggle been subsumed in the discourse of images, to the point that the struggle itself had been redefined, was now best understood in terms of the politics of perception, the struggle not to be totally subsumed in the play of commodities.

When Jill was gone Jack went back down to the bar and tried to get shit-faced. The music was really great and people were dancing. A very tall heavy-set blonde was in the corner dancing her head off. Jack got up and danced and quite soon found himself right beside her.

When the music stopped he said: Do you like Jim Morrison? And she said: Yeah, but I like Van Morrison better.

Jack found out that her name was Maureen, and he said if he

ever had kids he'd name his daughter Maureen, his favorite name. She said she'd never liked her name at all and was planning on changing it, maybe calling herself Marguerrite, or Mary Beth, or Melinda. Jack said he thought those names were good, but he liked Maureen much better. Maureen said she was tired of meeting guys with emotional problems, guys obsessed with self-help books and therapy, guys who couldn't accept their male identities. Jack wondered what she meant by "male identities." Maureen told him, going into meticulous detail, providing vivid examples and even defining all her terms. But Jack thought the whole idea was dumb. He said that he badly had to go to the men's room.

On his way to the men's room Jack bumped into his therapist, Bert, and his boss, Bart, holding hands and gazing into each other's eyes and laughing. He'd never suspected either one was gay, and they both looked embarrassed, mumbling a few inanely defensive remarks and then going out, walking quickly up the street, feeling as if their heads were about to float off into the ozone.

Bart was a thin, good-looking man from Tulsa. He'd come to New York in 1969, hoping to get his Ph.D. in psychology from Columbia, but he soon got knocked off course by an all-encompassing dislocation, by facts he could neither deny nor clearly describe. The motions by which mass commodities are multiplied in public space had already crossed the limits of their own abundance, and since the end of their uncontrolled reproduction was nowhere in sight, the situation had to be seen as a kind of enriched privation. At the moment of economic overproduction, the concentrated result of social control became quite visible, subjugating physical space to the play of invasive images, the interaction of which had produced the illusion of a culture. Words fell out of Bart's eyes and splashed in a pool of beer on the pavement. But Bert didn't care because Bert was a thin good-looking man from Tulsa too. He'd come to New York in 1972 to be a dancer. But there was too much competition, so he'd gone into psychotherapy instead, a move he now considered a big mistake, having been forced to confront all sorts of painful things that he couldn't resolve, like the fact that he hated successful people, that he had no time for his own mistakes, no time for the problems of others, that he couldn't stay hard when he cared about those he had sex with, that he stayed up late each night afraid that he might get obscene phone calls, that thunderclouds coming out of the south were certain signs of a loved-one's death, that vehement arguments made the world seem smaller, that Lot had sex with his daughters once his wife had been struck down, that his father once tried to kill the man who owned the world's third-largest pig, that his head felt like a balloon about to get popped at a birthday party.

The moon was romantic, poised above the silhouettes of buildings, as Bart and Bert walked arm in arm on Broadway toward Canal Street. But the mood was torn by the sound of a woman bitching out her husband, six flights up in a tenement near Chinatown, and her husband got really nasty, yelling abusively all the way down the staircase coming out on the street, where he threatened her with a butcher's knife, claiming she'd been unfaithful, calling her all sorts of obscene names, but then she lost her head, wrestling the knife away and knocking the man out cold with a quick left hook, not quite aware that the neighborhood had become completely expendable, reduced by the demands of commodified language, replaced by a sequence of images that existed above and beyond it, and which at the same time forced itself on the consciousness of the culture, presented as though it were nothing less than the tangible form of spatial events, at once both present and absent, like the book on TV wrestling that she stayed up late to finish, written by a guy who was clearly obsessed with domination, whose every word and phrase had masochistic implications, or at least that's what *she* thought, but she knew that she might be assuming too much, reading too much into a book not meant for careful analysis.

Still, she couldn't help thinking that everything had to be critically studied, that lots of the nonsense going on in the world looked harmless at first, but later turned out to be deadly, had to be checked out carefully, seen for what it really was and not for what it claimed to be, but then, she told herself, she'd always been too serious, suggesting perhaps that her own contradictions were little more than reflections of the struggles of power conglomerates, whose manufactured conflicts were really strategies of financial control, a means of diverting attention toward theatrical representations, away from the chaos and ruins that she found herself confined to, and suddenly she regretted having left her husband out cold on the street. She told herself it wasn't his fault. Then she told herself that it was. She told herself that it was again. And again. She began to believe it. He'd had no right to accuse her of being a prostitute, even if he hadn't really meant it, even if it had just been a figure of speech, because really figures of speech had lots of power, had been the cause of wars and great inventions, were at that very moment part of a marvelous performance, fifteen blocks downtown on Walker Street, Act One of *Hamlet*, the part where Polonius tells his son to give his thoughts no tongue, and Bill was dozing off in his front-row seat, feeling dumb because he'd gone out with a really bad cold and a fever. He had to keep gripping his chair to try not to break out in a spasm of coughing, and it stopped him from fully absorbing the play, making him feel even dumber. After all, the main reason he'd come was not because he liked Shakespeare, but because he had to read *Hamlet* for English 101 at NYU, and since he couldn't seem to get the hang of Shakespeare's language, he thought it might be better if he saw the play performed. No one else in his class could stand to read Shakespeare. All of them felt the language was too complex or too archaic. But they had a test coming up—they had to find some way to comprehend *Hamlet*. So Bill had come up with a plan. They'd all gone down to Walker Street with VCRs and notebooks. And now this cold was in the way. He tried but he couldn't grasp anything, and he fell back dazed in his chair, felt his fever increasing, dissolving into the spectacle of repressive pseudo-enjoyment, commodified representations of people employed as cultural icons, specious compensations, fraudulent satisfactions, all subsumed in the all-consuming rush of quantification. He vaguely sensed what others had already set aside as nonsense, that time has become a commodity, a pseudo-cyclical pattern simulating the very change it prevents, circulating because of the increased poverty it attempts to conceal, a poverty it creates and also perpetuates. Tradition and innovation are thus redefined as mere simulations, categories that only seem to refer to historical process, reproduced with a technological force not even the strong survive, making the future look like someone quitting her job without warning. He felt a big wind inside his body, felt it might get strong enough to rise and rip his head off.

But to put it that way was to make the wind seem to be little more than a figure of speech, when in truth it was really there blowing in every conceivable direction, driving his hair back off his face, knocking his teeth down his throat and tearing his head off, blowing his nose down the street. He sat there feeling stunned and stoned, like food getting cold at a wedding, or a baby left outside in cold November wind in a carriage, watching the world go by with no comprehension.

DOUBLE BED

Freddie might have been dead. Or he might have been trapped in sleep, the kind that's too complex to wake from. Or he might have been having the kind of dream you can't remember later, but which you nonetheless pretend to reconstruct from an image or two, building it into something a friend or therapist might find amusing. Or he might have been deep in stupor, plunging so firmly into an absence of mind that a vortex was forming, sucking him all the more firmly into a place his mind had abandoned. He might have been caught up in any one of these conditions, or all of them at once, as if several different possibilities were moving toward a more definite shape, and one of them took off in a totally unforeseen direction, and he suddenly found himself wide awake, staring at an unfamiliar woman stretched out naked beside him in bed.

Jenny opened her eyes two seconds later. She said: What are YOU doing here? And Freddie said: I live here, what are YOU doing here? Then they just stared at each other. Both felt the need to make a decisive argument, proving beyond all doubt whose double bed it really was, but neither felt up to the task, so they kept on staring. The light was ripping in through green silk drapes, thrusting in so fiercely that everything in the room, their faces and bodies included, seemed to be on the verge of becoming invisible. So both began to search in silent fear for explanations.

But only one explanation seemed at all plausible: that they both must have been really drunk in a single's bar the night before, picked each other up and gone to bed. Both of course had done this kind of thing many times in the past, so neither felt surprised. But the thought of having done it again was depressing, not because either one had moralistic inhibitions, but rather because they'd recently sworn off sex, and especially casual sex, having spent long nights with friends in hospitals dying of AIDS, and having gotten sick of going to bed with total strangers.

So they tried to find other reasons, not wanting to just admit that they'd been drunk and deeply horny, feeling like they were lost in a park in a dark and distant city, where children ran around screaming and fighting, and grown-ups thought their kids were cute for making so much noise, and a sky-blue hand was reaching down from a cardboard sky in the suburbs, and still no words came to mind so they kept on staring, not moving, barely breathing, completely oblivious to the loud knocking at the door, a sound that should have made it clear to both Jenny and Freddie that city life is an architectural discourse, a language in three dimensions, and we therefore need to prepare a careful response in three dimensions, a durably installed generative principle of regulated improvisations, aware that the ethics of disposability clearly signify more than merely throwing out plastic spoons and forks, but in fact refer to the disposability of moral values, of personalities, relationships with other people, relationships between people and what they perceive, the values they might assign to space and time and material objects, producing in the long run a kind of paralysis, a depressive condition in which all things appear inaccessible, but also desirable, and nothing seems clear. But Freddie was pretty clear about one thing, something which made his earlier thoughts about how he'd ended up with Jenny seem completely ridiculous, and this one thing was that he had no recollection, not even the vaguest memory, of having been looking for sex the night before. Nor did Jenny look even slightly familiar. She didn't even remind him of his mother.

Jenny put her finger in his mouth, smiled as if his dick might be a light green rubber duck, tried to get a romantic look in her eyes. But none of it came off with any conviction. And Freddie's response was painfully mechanical, as if he could tell she was just going through the motions, initiating sex because their proximity seemed to suggest it. In fact, it suggested a good deal more, a matrix of implications that became painfully clear when the room was suddenly filled with a horrible sound coming out of the north, a long sound gripping and stretching the sky, ripping the stitches that held it together, but no indication of what the sound was, and no sense that anyone else—anyone in rooms nearby or anyone out on the street—was even in the vaguest way aware of it.

Jenny creased her brow. Freddie wasn't sure what she meant,

so he creased his brow in response, put his finger in her mouth, then took it out and wiped it on his thigh. Jenny smiled and began to moan, rubbing her teeth against his neck. Both could hear the sound of people walking past on the pavement. They tried to pay close attention to that sound, tracing it up and down the street, footsteps coming close and moving away, but the truth is that control over information, coupled with an instant capacity for analyzing huge amounts of data, is crucial in coordinating far-flung corporate interests, as if to say that history can now be seen as a vast archive filled with instantly retrievable events, each of which can be consumed and reconsumed at the push of a button. Time is nothing more than a costume drama. By treating certain idealized conceptions of space and time as if they were physically real, we run the risk of confining the free flow of human experience to a set of rational expectations. Our thinking starts to look, in fact, like a motel struck by lightning.

So Freddie said, Why don't we get up and have breakfast? Maybe we could have a conversation.

And Jenny said, Yeah, sure, that sounds good. We could talk about our favorite TV shows, and from there we could move into something more intimate, like how our parents messed us up, and how we've had to spend thousands of dollars on therapy. The gnashing sunlight forced its way through the blinds onto Freddie's forehead, making his face appear to be sliced into three unequal sections, but Jenny thought his face had been sliced into five unequal sections, and she thought she might tell him that, in no uncertain terms, until that thought was replaced by a thought that had twelve equal sections, and then collapsed in a heap at the foot of the bed.

The knocking at the door got louder and louder, as if it were slowly building toward a point of no return, a crescendo of sorts that would finally reveal, in pure non-verbal terms, the unequivocal meaning of what they were doing there, assuming such unequivocal terms could really be brought into focus. After all, what appears at first unequivocal, needing no explanation, may suddenly seem offensively complex in the face of new information. The collapse of money as means of firmly representing value, like a train breaking down before leaving the station, has led to a widespread crisis of representation. The rapidity with which currency markets fluctuate, for example, may well define a larger fluctuation, a shift in how we approach our basic spatial situation. Time horizons collapse, birds get bored and stop flying, the footsteps on the pavement seem to get louder moving farther away. Even as recently as fifteen years ago, we might have appealed to a standardized sense of space and time as a point of departure. But today things are quite different, and on some days that difference becomes unavoidable, and Freddie and Jenny felt that difference keenly, and the sun was coming in like a battering ram, like an angry fullback bashing in for a touchdown, like a Bengal tiger smashing through a fancy storefront window, like someone stuffing your mouth with a huge potato.

So many things were happening all at once, and Freddie felt the need to get some firmly defined information. He fixed his gaze on Jenny's lovely neck and showed his big sharp teeth. Then he asked her if she liked modern dance and she said that she did, that in fact she'd done modern dance for fifteen years before messing up her back, and he said he could tell she'd been a dancer because she was all curve and muscle, a phrase he'd meant as a turn-on, but she took it the wrong way since it reminded her that no matter how beautiful her body was it hadn't helped her find the right person to settle down with, and now she was almost too old to have kids, but Freddie thought that kids were a pain in the ass, and besides, why bring kids into a doomed and disgracefully unfair world, but this made Jenny sad again, because she knew that unless people had kids the human species would come to an end, so Freddie said that he prided himself on being honest enough to admit that he didn't care if humanity came to an end, and that he didn't think people who said they cared were better people than he was just because they felt the need to say what they thought other people expected, but Jenny said she didn't think it had anything to do with expectations, she said it had more to do with convictions, and the steeple clock outside began to chime, it was nearly ten, and the knocking at the door was getting louder, and someone outside began screaming, but nothing seemed to penetrate the basin of attraction, bland and unfocused though it might have been, that hovered above the bed in the churning sunlight. This was the bitter harvest of charismatic politics, of voodoo economics, of passive depictions of otherness, of people getting drunk at cocktail parties, of born-again

Christians getting hooked on pornographic movies, of people going mad from having too much time to kill.

But Jenny knew how to brush past what she recognized as nonsense, and she knew how to penetrate, how to use her hands to gently open a person's body, to form a gap in his flesh and pull it wide, climb inside, stay there until it was safe to come out—a good thing to know how to do, except that with Freddie she felt no need to be cautious. It wasn't that he was so gentle or sensitive or anything like that, but that he was preoccupied, concerned that money was quickly becoming totally fictitious, reducing all significance to a rubble of obsolete sounds and shapes, a lunar landscape not unlike Hiroshima, or a burning face, or stepping on someone's dog by mistake, or doing it on purpose. The days were becoming the past before they were fully part of the present, and Freddie said: What came from my hands allows me to see your face, and Jenny looked puzzled, but she didn't want to get stuck staring in silence again, so she said they should go out for breakfast, talk about how their parents had messed up their childhoods, skip the talk about their favorite TV shows and movies, get married in a fancy modern chapel, and then decide about having kids, or maybe get a dog instead, decide on what kind later. But Freddie put on a big smile, ran his fingers up her shapely thigh, sucked her shoulder, played with her so gently, so skillfully, and in the end with such abandon, that soon she began to split with unrehearsed passion, gripping the sides of the bed and staring her way through the wall toward a cardboard sky, grunting like someone making repairs on a highway into the future. And when she came, the knocking stopped, the footsteps on the pavement stopped, the chimes from the nearby steeple stopped. The street grew dark and violent.

NATIONAL DISASTER

Those who live in New York and take the trains will no doubt have seen her. She's an utterly stunning Hispanic woman posing in lavishly photographed color, lovely light brown skin against a swirling pale blue background. She looks at you with an irresistible Mona Lisa face, holding your gaze, making it seem as if she's there for you alone, throwing her ample chest out barely contained by a bright red skin-tight gown, supple arms reaching up in back of her head, shades with bright green lenses tilted back up into her long black hair. The contrast between the green of her shades and the red of her gown is perfect, and since the lenses seem to be opaque, it's clear that they're in the picture solely to serve as decorations, solely to compel your eyes, to make them blind with passion, or perhaps to suggest that you've got the green light, she's available for your pleasure—even though she's clearly not, it's all a tease, just a picture. Above her you find the words: *Set Your Sights on Ballantine Beer*. And of course there's a really big bottle of Ballantine Beer in the picture beside her.

George was a pretty smart guy with a Ph.D. in psycho-linguistics. He was on the train one day when the ad caught his eye. There was no turning back. Though he deeply detested the cheap manipulations of Madison Avenue—the games they played with human desire and perception—and often refused to even look at advertising images, he found himself in love with the way this woman completely absorbed his attention. From that day on, he always tried to find her on the subway, often walking from car to car, finally sitting down across from her face and her well-displayed body. At times, he might open a book, pretend to be reading. But soon he would find himself staring, lost in her look, thrilled with her body, a feeling made all the more intense by the fact that he wasn't an idiot. He knew the ad was designed to seduce him, a carefully manufactured effect, that in fact it relied on persuasion techniques that over the years had been widely critiqued, that it seemed so extreme that it had to be some sort of joke, a kind of strategic attack, laughing at academic efforts to blunt its hypnotic effect, laughing at feminist arguments against using women to sell things. None of it made any difference. He'd never known himself to be so delightfully overwhelmed. He prayed every day to meet this woman, perhaps at a party or bar, and before too long his prayers were deliciously answered.

A friend of his had a friend who worked at a midtown modeling agency, and when George mentioned the ad his friend said his friend knew the woman quite well, and knew she would soon be attending a party George could also attend. George was nervous at first, but his friend got him drunk, and the rest was no problem. They got there a minute before she walked in, sporting precisely the same red skin-tight gown, the same Mona Lisa face.

He said: Haven't I seen you before?

She said: I guess I'm hard to miss.

He said: Do you really like Ballantine Beer?

She made a face: It's disgusting!

The woman's name was probably Milagros. Or it might have been Maxine or Michelle, or perhaps Roxanne, or Rebecca. The ambiguity seemed completely appropriate, somehow seemed to complement the bright green shades in her long black hair, so George thought his name for the night might just as well be Dick or Johnny. They went to her room. The papered walls had a pale-blue swirling pattern. Beside her magnificent bed was an eight-foot bottle of Ballantine Beer.

He stared at the bottle and said: What's *this* all about?

She took his face in her hands and said: It's an emblem of your passion—larger than life, erect with foam and pleasure, up until now bottled up. Just open the bottle so both of us can drink! And she took him down under the sheets, doing whatever he thought she did until dawn and the bottle was empty.

Johnny-George got to know Maxine-Milagros really well. The games they played with their names were quite in line with the tone of the times, an outgrowth of the fact that words aren't rooted in what they refer to, that language can only be seen as a pattern of differences, that what people say to each other is unavoidably filled with distortions, verbal conventions that make people seem to be close when they're really distant. Nonetheless, they were doing quite well, serious talks and powerful sex, until one day there were giant ants in Nigeria, fifteen people freaking out on LSD in the White House, twenty-nine crates of liquid paper getting bombed in the Caspian Sea, mad dogs on the prowl outside Soweto, fingers getting chopped off in a bar near Saõ Paulo, eighty-five clowns discovered in a mass grave south of Topeka, hundreds of college professors forgetting how to play chess in Georgia, all of this accompanied by changes in her face, inexplicable transformations that made her begin to look like him, made it seem as if she'd never been more than a reflection, as if her bright green shades had always been blocking out the look in her eyes, no longer merely opaque but functioning now like twin green mirrors, and on that day their love was declared a national disaster.

FAKE MURDERS

On May 28 at 5 p.m. Dave Dean, dressed in designer jeans, a souvenir t-shirt from Yellowstone Park and a New York Yankees baseball hat, broke into a small motel room near Birmingham, Alabama. There he found his wife Michelle in bed with her lover Daisy. He pulled out the gun he'd bought a few days back in preparation. He wanted to say something witty, deeply sarcastic, even profound, before he blew them both away. But he found himself inarticulate. He stood there working hard to think of the gangster films he'd seen, the clever lines that charismatic tough guys always delivered, but the words wouldn't come. He looked at his gun. He felt like he might want to bite off his tongue. He put a really mean smile on his face, prepared to pull the trigger. They looked up from the bed in rage and terror. The room was all pressure. They felt like they might be trapped inside a balloon that was just about to get popped. The moment split, moving in several directions, each at a different speed, some going up and some going down, some getting large, some dissolving.

But the truth was Bob had no idea that something like this was taking place. Or if he did he kept it to himself. He made no sign of it. Indeed, he was caught up in something else, driving toward Nebraska, the Rocky Mountains fading into the dark of his rearview mirror. He knew that Orson Bates was in Lincoln, Nebraska. He knew that Orson Bates had raped his daughter back in December. He knew that Orson Bates had gotten off easy because the judge was a pig, a one-time rapist himself, though nobody mentioned it. So Bob was going to make Orson pay. He'd find out where he took his meals, his favorite spot, and when he was there. He'd walk in looking like someone else, a fake white beard, dark glasses, and Orson would look up and see him but have no reaction. Bob would sit three tables away, seem to look at the menu, glance at the walls, papered with tiny homesteads on the prairie. The overhead fans would turn slowly through their own shadows. Then it would happen. Bob would clear his throat and pound on the table. He'd loudly call Orson a rapist, meeting his eyes with pent-up anger, repeating the charge even louder when he tried to look away. Bob would pull out his gun, savor the panic in Orson's face, ignoring the scream of the waitress, the sound of a train going by down the block, the silhouettes of weather vanes on the nearby mansard housetops. The moment would vanish into the moment that followed it. The moment would swallow itself by the tail, connecting itself with all moments to come, as if they'd somehow kept what they contained—their own special motions, the shapes and colors that made them unique—yet they'd all become interchangeable.

But none of them would change anything. The sun would still come in through the blue silk drapes in the elegant brownstone, where a woman dressed in a polka-dot skirt, reading the morning paper, would lean toward her husband and say: Hey Ken! According to this new poll, ninety-six percent of the American people believe that the polls have no statistical validity whatsoever! And Ken would say: Gee, Bonnie! If that's what the people think, then it must be true. But he wouldn't quite get through the sentence. A man he'd fired five months before would have already come through the window, leaping in from the fire escape, a blow torch in his hand, moving slowly across the lovely old carpeting in the shadows, Bonnie grabbing Ken's arm but no words coming out of her mouth.

But more important concerns quickly had to be reckoned with. In a world in which making sense no longer makes any sense, and in truth never did, does it make any sense to make nonsense, and make it as though it made sense? The truth was clear. Jim could best be described as oddly punitive. He'd always been that way, though in the past people couldn't describe him. He stood stark naked, carefully concealed in Melanie's closet. Soon he heard her voice, and the voice of her analyst, coming in through the door. Then he heard them collapse on the bed, passionate loud kissing, zippers getting unzipped, pants getting pulled off, shirts getting tossed on the floor. He waited until the moaning began. Then he jumped out into the darkness, aiming the beam of his flashlight into their squinting eyes, looking wild with his knife. Melanie had said she wanted some time to be on her own, to sort some deep confusions

THE GOTHIC TWILIGHT

out. She'd wanted to work with an analyst. But word had gotten back to Jim that she'd gotten more than analysis. So he stood there with his flashlight and his knife and said: Well, Mr. Freud, if this were a dream, what would what I'm holding be symbolic of? And he laughed and laughed, having so much fun that he nearly forgot what he was there for, that he nearly forgot his own rage, that all discrete things need to be parts of a systematic arrangement, a universe of patterns to make them function according to how they're made, to supply their requisite status, just as every statement describing a fact must also propose a clear pattern, a context within which what that fact reveals can seem to make sense, which means that logical propositions, even if they make no claim to universal truth, can nonetheless embody a partial truth, a claim whose truth is determined by the system it's contained by, a system fully presupposed in the proposition's meaning.

But Linda Jones had other things on her mind. She knew that the man she'd interviewed with was a total sexist pig, that even though she'd had all the qualifications for the job, he'd hired another woman because of her looks, because she was sexy, because she was willing to stroke his male insecurity during the interview. Linda knew that this kind of thing was rampant in the business world, that the man was really no worse than a hundred thousand other male bosses. But Linda felt it was time to make a statement. She stood outside the man's office until he was there by himself in the twilight. She walked in without knocking, dropped her skirt, threw her blouse off, and told him to get on his knees, waving a baseball bat in warning. She made commands in a voice that she'd been practicing for more than a week, telling him to put his face between her thighs and do his thing, and just as he moved in close she used her knee to knock his teeth out. She heard the police pull up outside with a group of excited reporters. She'd called the papers ten minutes before to explain her motivations, making sure that the man's death wouldn't in any way be misinterpreted, that in the future men would think more than twice about sexist agendas. She knew it was time to finish the job with her bat, that even her own best friends might be imposters, that all known forms of perfection seem accidental, that answers that don't beg the questions aren't really answers, that the line between tautologies and empirical generalizations, far from comprising the basis of pure mathematics, can't be sharply drawn, that past and future converge on a place that's already gone by the time they arrive, that until she finished him off she would never quite know what it meant to be fully alive.

But finding her way in the dark was more complex than she'd imagined. Daisy drove with her headlights off down the dead-end street in silence. She didn't want anyone waking up and hearing screams next door. But she'd never tried to drive in the dark before, so she finally got out and walked. Soon she was in his basement, moving up one step at a time, careful not to let any sounds escape from the old wooden staircase. Then she was outside the bedroom door, where Dave was making love with his wife Michelle, her part-time lover. Right before they were both about to come, she burst inside, shooting out the lights on the matching tables on either side of the bed, asking Michelle if she liked it better with guys. Michelle sort of laughed in surprise, a response that quickly gave way to rage and terror. But Dave, who always made love with a baseball hat on his head, knew just what to say. He sounded sarcastic, witty, profound, just like a TV gangster—just as Daisy smiled and pulled the trigger.

THE KING OF NOISE

One loud spring day, Kenneth Barnes was jailed for noise pollution. As president of a company that made garbage trucks and busses, several famous lines of motorcycles, and served as chief distributor for companies that made fire trucks, horns and alarms for cars, ambulance and police car sirens, he was found guilty of public negligence, of not taking steps to reduce the abusive noise his products made. He claimed, of course, that such steps would have cost him too much time and money. But in a series of heated courtroom battles—where lawyers paraded their eloquence on unprecedented levels—his claim was found unacceptable, and soon he was sent from his prison cell to a noise reprogramming center.

After a few initial tests, he found himself the subject of experimental procedures, adjustments in his neurological patterning, that left him completely intolerant of sirens and horns of any kind. The hideous grinding sounds of sanitation trucks drove him crazy, and when he heard macho bikers racing their engines, filling the streets with all the noise they were capable of producing, he no longer told himself that at least they weren't out raping their mothers; he told himself they ought to be sent to noise castration centers. After a year of intense and painful treatment, Kenneth Barnes was eager to mend his ways, to put all his time and money into noise reduction research. He was given two years by the State to make his products more humane, quiet enough so that he himself—in his new noise-hating condition—could tolerate whatever sounds they made.

Meanwhile, Tara Shapiro, Kenneth Barnes's young fiancée, had decided to break their engagement. She wanted no more connection with someone whose noise had done so much to pollute so many urban spaces. She'd heard, of course, that he'd changed his tune at the noise reprogramming center, but she had no faith in his powers of endurance. She was pretty sure that soon he'd again be making money by selling noise. Besides, after five long years of intense group therapy, she no longer found herself looking for men who'd sold their souls to the system. She wanted guys with brains, or lacking brains, artistic integrity.

At a party she unexpectedly ran into Dick McLeary, an old acquaintance who'd recently gotten married. She'd always thought Dick was cute but had never felt free enough to approach him. And she'd always suspected that Dick was really interested, or at least physically attracted, but he'd never had the nerve to speak directly. Besides, Dick was a painter who did temp typing to make ends meet, and she'd always taken pains to seem like a woman who wanted money. But now, she told herself, she saw the world through different eyes, and besides, Dick was married now, unavailable. She thought she could say what she felt without fear of seeming too inviting, without Dick becoming assertive about what she assumed he desired.

Hey Dick, she said, I've been meaning to ask you: How come you never asked me out a few years back when we were in group therapy together?

He stood there secretly thrilled, amazed, not quite sure what to say, as if the glass he was drinking from was filled with tropical fish. He'd never dreamed that a woman like Tara would go for a starving painter like him, and though at times he tried to think of himself as attractive to women, for the most part he felt that his physical appearance was nothing special, that she would have politely found ways of not going out with him, like saying that she liked him as a friend but not as a lover, especially since at the time she was starting to get involved with Kenneth Barnes, a widely photographed man-about-town with a legendary income.

Working hard to sound calm, he said: Well, you know, I'm kind of shy about that sort of thing, and besides, you were involved, weren't you? I mean, you always talked in therapy about how hard it was to be in love with the King of Noise. Wasn't that what you called Ken Barnes? The King of Noise?

She laughed and put her hands on his flabby waist and pressed it lightly. Through the window the violent noise of a big bike tore down the avenue, followed by a loud car alarm going off, then the sound of an ambulance, slowly fading into the distance just as the horrid whine of the number ten bus approached, then a fire truck siren, quickly moving closer until it stopped outside the window. The firemen aimed big searchlights into the room, shouting urgent instructions through megaphones, pulling out hoses, shooting savage jets of freezing water up toward the party. Dick and Tara gripped each other in terror. A look of terminal passion filled their eyes.

The next day Kenneth Barnes read the morning papers over toast and tea, fantasizing about new noise abuse reduction procedures. A story about a big fire on East 23rd Street caught his eye. There were detailed descriptions of damage, a party of thirty people, all of whom had died in the blaze, a fire apparently started when someone forgot that his oven was on, or at least that's what the doorman said, and the King of Noise felt weird. As he tried to imagine the scene of the fire, fire truck sirens played on the edge of his mind and began moving closer. Soon the sound was obscene. Hands on his ears, he ran to the window.

He opened his mouth and the sound sprayed violently out all over the neighborhood, bouncing off nearby windows behind which Bob and Marci played parchesi, munching fritos and onion dip, planning revolution, and the sound was dropping down to the street, where Bonnie Smith made eyes at the sandwich man at the corner deli, and the sandwich man thought Bonnie was getting ready to steal his twinkies, and the sound shot down the street, around the corner, pressed on a shopfront, where a manikin stared straight into the savage early morning sunlight, and the chic new gown it was modeling glowed and seemed to be covered with ketchup, and the sound went down a dark alleyway beside an abandoned hardware store, stroking Brandon's cheekbones, making new holes in his tattered shoes, waking him up in the massive pile of trash he'd gone to sleep on, and the sound bounced back and forth on a fancy street of facing brownstones, stripping all the trees, turning the falling leaves into mirrors, and the sound slipped in through an open window facing an old museum, shattering a fishbowl, knocking old portraits down off the walls, leaving all the doorknobs cold as ice for twenty-five minutes, and the sound cut back outside, assailing pigeons perched on a window ledge, driving them out of their senses, leaving them unsure how to fly, and the

THE KING OF NOISE

sound bashed into a group of tall condominiums, bending the steel and rock and glass and iron that held them together, leaving them shaped like weird mathematical symbols. The sound circled back, returned to its source, got caught in a feedback loop, increasing in volume, distorting, starting back out into the city, and it would have kept going forever, except that within maybe fifteen minutes police cars came with flashing lights, carving up the morning air with the noise their sirens projected.

They bound the King of Noise and gagged him securely, booking him at the station for noise pollution, for disturbing the peace, and soon he was back at the noise reprogramming center for more severe treatments, raving from his dreams that a guy named Dick had been fucking his girlfriend.

THE FRENCH REVOLUTION

Waking up early one morning in late September, 1783, finding himself with nothing to do and feeling a trace of anxiety, Anthony Mesmer magnetized his gardener. He watched him assume a trancelike state, a condition that Mesmer knew involved a suspension of sight and hearing, accompanied by an inward amplification of thought and feeling, to such an extent that all the outward senses became unimportant, replaced by warm fluids that carried the brain in several directions at once, and it was through these fluids that Mesmer began to question his friend.

The gardener seemed to know everything that Mesmer wanted to know. Answers came like dark stone rooms in facing floorlength mirrors. Reflections put each room inside itself, outside itself, as if the carpets and tables and chairs no longer had any substance, as if they were nothing more than a means of duplicating themselves. Time disappeared in the replication of moonlight on the floorboards, in tossing white silk drapes and mirrored casements. The verbal suggestions that usually frame an answer began to advance and recede, coming closer and moving away in multiplied reflections.

The only limits were those of the questions Mesmer was able to pose, and here initial complications began. Since what the gardener said could only come out in response to questions, the burden was placed on Mesmer to know precisely what he was after, to know in advance the approximate range of response that the gardener might provide, and this made the gardener's answers too predictable. What Mesmer thought he was looking for no longer held his interest, and boredom might have ensued. But it soon became clear that things were changing. With each replication, the dark stone rooms became smaller, yet each on its own scale seemed to be complete with carpets and tables and chairs, meaning that each new response the gardener provided suggested a new set of questions, and each new question suggested a whole new framework of response, a whole new scale of perception, complete with tossing drapes and mirrors.

Mesmer was soon convinced that his gardener's soul had been greatly enlarged, empowered by the magnetic fluids that brought him sense impressions direct from the outside world, without interference, without the dilution that always occurs when the brain is involved in perception, and Mesmer could see in his gardener a great potential source of magic, a depth of communion with nature very few people even dream of. After a time, he began to converse with his gardener without language, directly exchanging magnetic sensations without using words for translation, moving beyond the complex filter of verbal representation, moving beyond all the metaphors, the dark stone replications.

Soon it was clear that Mesmer could also magnetize rocks and blocks of wood. He expanded his practice to branches and leaves, then the trunks of the trees and the roots. And before too long, in silent magnetic interchange with his gardener, Mesmer concluded that he could make use of a tree to perform special services, that a magnetized tree might well become a source of healing and dreaming. He thought of the giant elm on the village green, beneath which buxom peasant girls often danced on festive occasions, and old men relaxed, drinking their *vin du pays* on fine summer evenings. Mesmer sized up the tree, ran his hands up and down its magnificent bark, carefully projecting streams of warm magnetic fluid, guiding it into the branches and leaves, down the trunk to the roots and finally into the dense green grass. He filled the shade beneath its massive boughs with small wooden tables and chairs, where the townspeople sat while Mesmer connected their wounds to the tree with magnetized rope. They closed their eyes and held each other's hands in a magic circle, drinking in the magnetic pulse that flowed up and down from the branches and roots, put them in touch with the photosynthetic motions of the leaves, in touch with the circles of strength and time in the trunk of the tree, cooling off in the shade. Soon they felt normal, cured, and more than that, they had moved beyond language. The painful distortions of verbal representation disappeared, had no meaning inside their circle of strength and its nurturing silence.

But one day Mesmer made a crucial mistake, badly misinterpreting the gardener's dream of a talking giraffe. The gardener had never seen a giraffe before, so when it appeared in his dream he really had no idea what it was. All he could do was provide a vague description, forcing images into the shape of a narrative, a verbal construction that had very little to do with what he'd been dreaming. Instead of sharing unfiltered magnetic sensations, Mesmer and his gardener fell back into words, into representations, and things got really messed up. Mesmer assumed the giraffe was an elephant, even though he'd never been within five hundred miles of an elephant, had never even seen a sketch, though he may have heard a description or two.

So basing his thoughts on an animal shape he'd never seen and knew nothing about, Mesmer spoke in a fake trance telling the gardener to take his own life, insisting that dreams about elephants clearly meant that death was approaching, a slow and painful death, the kind that made suicide seem attractive. When the gardener hung himself it broke the trance of the tree completely. The people wanted Mesmer's blood. They came with torches and pitchforks. But he'd already caught the midnight coach, arriving in Paris just before dawn on New Year's Day, 1784, and before too long he became the rage of Paris.

He set himself up in a lovely house on the Left Bank facing the Seine, where stained glass windows gave his black stone rooms a feeling of limitless depth, a dreamy sensation that multiplied itself in a hundred mirrors. Incense burned in antique urns on a mantelpiece in each chamber, and a very sweet female voice from somewhere above or below sang faintly, a lovely melodic pattern repeating itself in variations, over and over again, delightfully subtle in its changes.

In the central salon was a huge black oval cauldron, a vessel of magnetized water that people applied to their wounds, drifting into a trance, losing themselves in an atmosphere that distilled their thoughts and feelings, setting the stage for mesmerizing sensations. Dressed in a purple silk robe embroidered richly with bright gold flowers, waving a white magnetic wand, a look of pensive dignity on his firm and well-prepared face, Mesmer came out of the mirroring dark. He moved his wand on their bodies, tracing a biochemical map, shaping their internal energies with intense magnetic projections. Hot and cold vapours changed their positions,

THE FRENCH REVOLUTION

humours became reconditioned, leaving the sick and wounded greatly changed and seemingly cured, anatomically redesigned, not sure where they'd been or what they'd become, but feeling better.

Mesmer's fame spread out from Paris and France. He was known throughout Europe. Though his cures were incomplete and rarely lasted more than a week, his name became a household word. He became good friends with Marie Antoinette. Everyone seemed to believe what he said. But soon he had competition.

Benjamin Douglas Perkins, an American who'd argued against the ideas of the Founding Fathers, refusing to sign their Declaration back in 1776, appeared in Paris practicing magnetic transformation, working with what he called Metallic Tractors. By placing blocks of metal on a wound and moving them gently, Perkins magnetized hundreds of people in weeks all over the city. Rheumatism was quickly cured. Toothaches disappeared. People with gout forgot their pains within minutes. Since Perkins cleverly kept his price quite low, at least at first, Mesmer's business declined. His reputation seemed to be fading. He knew he'd have to be quick in driving out the competition.

So he got a friend from Britain, Dr. Haygarth, a man who was widely known as a court astrologer, to come to France with fake Metallic Tractors, healing people all over the city, getting lots of attention, then publishing a report that the Tractors were nothing but small blocks of wood, that they had no magnetic powers at all, that the people he'd healed had only been transformed in their minds, not their bodies, that he'd only been trying to demonstrate that Perkins was a phoney, that the people he'd cured had been actors hired to simulate improved health. Mesmer made sure the report appeared in several major papers. Word spread quickly and soon the city was filled with magnetized anger. The people Perkins had cured were up in arms. They were suddenly sick again. They began to imagine symptoms worse than those they'd first been cured of. Perkins knew that he'd better be quick. He knew there would soon be torches and pitchforks. He left in disguise, got back to the States, settling down with millions, a grand estate by the sea in Maine, a sick French wife and a fake name.

Mesmer's fame returned, but he knew that he'd better get out while he could. Debates in the Paris academies raged, and most of them went against him. After all, he got quick results, and the process of treatment was fun, filled with atmospheric pleasures and mysteries, magic language. The doctors looked at their methods and felt really boring, felt their work was in doubt. Mesmer knew they would soon find a way to make him look like a charlatan. Then all hell would break loose. He'd end up in jail or facing a noose.

Sitting among his mirrors in the darkness, Mesmer pondered his future, not at all sure where to go, or what to do. He sat there quite a long time before he asked himself the right question. The answer began when he faced himself in the glass, looking back from the darkness, projecting magnetic fluid into his image, his image in the mirror projecting the fluid back into his eyes, his eyes projecting the fluid back into the mirror. The motion back and forth could have gone on forever, suggesting that the imagination can't be confined in space and time, that it has a kind of wild, pre-civilized quality, and first evolved at a time when the human mind was forced to be cunning and fierce, matching wits with nature to survive. But nature in 1784 seemed rather tame, had been so for years, and the human imagination was no longer pushed to be so savage, indeed had become rather flabby, often taking degraded forms in politics and commerce. And yet it remained—in those who felt estranged from the web of convention—a mode of transgression, the source of delight in perversion, a fountain of healing and words, the path beyond words, a more-than-rational mode of apperception.

When authorities finally knocked on Mesmer's door maybe six weeks later—his good friend Haygarth finally beginning to wonder why Mesmer had been out of touch—they found only magnetized mirrors keeping the rooms in place in the darkness. Five years later, the French Revolution began.

OPERATION WELCOME HOME
(for Marc Kaminsky)

> "Look for me in the whirlwind"
> —Marcus Garvey

Confetti was pouring down everywhere like acid rain on Wall Street. Panzer divisions were grinding over the pavement. The street was filled with American flags and beaming suburban housewives, pot-bellied husbands wearing brand-new Norman Schwarzkopf t-shirts. Schwarzkopf raised his arms and the sea of noise became dead silence. His words made a gap in time. Everyone quickly became hard of hearing, hard of thinking, hard of talking, hard of feeling, hard in their hearts of darkness, and the horror spread and quickly seemed as normal as breath or a heartbeat, hiding itself in a million smiling teeth and bright unfocused eyes, or outlets for designer jeans polluting an African river, Columbus driven mad with bad arthritis, a bar of soap in an empty apartment causing a year of bad luck in Algiers, or someone forgetting to save a rock star's autograph. The huge clouds over the buildings quickly became stone cows and plastic pigs, and there was fake lightning, a huge queen of hearts impaled on the Gothic spire of the Trinity Church, and reams of patriotic trash, confetti floating like fallout, a new Manhattan Project, as prepubescent boys and girls got hooked on crack in the projects.

The newsman got there just in time to get a great front page picture, except that he'd forgotten his film, and besides, he was tired of front page news, or news of any kind. He was planning to quit and go to Central America, try to soothe his conscience doing social work or teaching, so he didn't care if he got fired for incompetence, for failing to get a picture of people screaming and throwing confetti, the very same picture all the other papers would print in their morning editions. He was really there to meet a woman, and he quickly found one, a college sophomore with a Patriot missile t-shirt, and soon they were in a bar near Battery Park, hands on each other's thighs beneath a white formica table, getting bombed on Bud while Schwarzkopf made quick work of the nation, smiling for network footage, for feature stories in *People*, or *New York* magazine, and the college sophomore said she might be a journalist herself some day, go to Nicaragua, do volunteer work for *La Prensa*, but the newsman said he was tired of just collecting facts and figures, knowing that he could only report what his editor felt was fit to print. He said that he wanted to be his own boss, get famous doing social work in Panama, then write it all up in a series of articles published in *The New Yorker*, work out a big book contract he could live on for the rest of his life, giving writing workshops from time to time at Breadloaf, and the clouds became iridescent blue in the floodlights over Schwarzkopf's head, and the sophomore felt like a shopping cart overturned in mud near the Brooklyn Bridge, or nineteen ex-G.I.s dozing off in the shade of a roadside billboard, a nicely-told strategic lie at a senior prom in Bridgeport, a day just like any other day becoming slightly different, a corporate resumé burned in a wild satanic mass in Tashkent, a schoolboy getting Marco Polo mixed up with Columbus, a snapping turtle getting filmed for use in a porno movie, or the Goodyear blimp crashing into the World Trade Center.

Schwarzkopf tried to look serious for the cameras, but his face was like a map of Outer Mongolia, or like a punctured football covered with insects, a nose in his mouth and a mouth in each eye, a beard where his nose should have been, big white teeth in place of his ears, jutting out like wings of ice, dripping and finally flowing down his neck in the hot summer sunlight. He had the look of someone who might have had horseflies buzzing around his head, a constant noise in his ears, even though his ears were melting.

He said: Longer ago than I care to remember, right after summer boot camp at West Point, I swallowed a frog on a bet, swallowed him whole and alive and croaking. For more than a week, he stayed alive and sang inside my belly. Night and day, I could feel him flipping around with his little webbed feet. For some folks, I imagine, it might have seemed quite gruesome. But I'm here to say

OPERATION WELCOME HOME

that I don't regret it one bit. It was all really worth it. Even today, I think of that frog each time I sit at my desk and try to put my thoughts on paper. A strange connection, some might think, but even if I try to sign my own name—a name that more than anything else in this world allows me to be who I am—deeply conflicting forces work in my wrist and hand and fingers. And if I try to work toward more complex forms of expression—a sentence perhaps, or a paragraph—something inside me tries to unwrite each word. And something tries to unspeak or unthink each word I speak, each thought I think. It's a wonder that I can speak and think at all, and it keeps getting harder.

The general's words were drowned in massive applause all over Manhattan, but the newsman kept on drinking, resting his hand in the sophomore's crotch, and she was too drunk to notice or get turned on, and the newsman was too drunk to know she was too drunk to notice or get turned on. The jukebox played non-stop drowning out nine-tenths of what they said, and the rest became bad dreams about someone's father, became the titles of books about how to stop dating the wrong kinds of people, captions for magazine photos of dolphins washing up dead on the Jersey shore, dialogue in a Boris Karloff movie, left wing anti-war slogans used out of context on the five o'clock news, or the words of a famous neurosurgeon beating his wife in Duluth.

Schwarzkopf's beaming face disappeared in a maelstrom of confetti. Schwarzkopf's radiant face dissolved in a blizzard of confetti. Schwarzkopf's luminous face got lost in a whirlwind of confetti. So look for Schwarzkopf in the whirlwind, in the new Madonna video, in ads for TV dinners, baseball bats or modular phones, on bowls and plates in motel snack-bars coast-to-coast, in brothels, in Brussels getting bombed with media moguls, in biographies, in billion-dollar cigarette publicity campaigns, on bubble-gum cards of Operation Desert Storm in drugstores.

Or on the TV screen of a cheezy bar near Battery Park, where the sophomore came to the brink of blowing lunch between slurred bits of speech. But the newsman got a second wind, became lucid, made the connections, imagined the massacred bodies carefully kept away from the five o'clock news, Desert Storm balloons going up and each with a dead face gazing down, the celebrating millions lifting souvenir flags to the souvenir sky, each like a scrap of

45

THE GOTHIC TWILIGHT

newsprint caught in a whirlwind, each one hoping to be a background face on the five o'clock news, and the newsman said he thought the whole thing was pathetic, utterly sickening, that he himself was pathetic, utterly sickening. The sophomore creased her brow and tried to look sensitive, then vomited, messing up her Patriot missile t-shirt, making the newsman think of a walkman getting squashed by a big mack truck, Mighty Mo in the Persian Gulf unloading death into south Iraq, wallets getting cooked and served as hamburgers on Beacon Hill, Francis Bacon crucified in new-age physics textbooks, a homeless woman told to stop asking for change and look for a job for a change, a thousand cursing drivers honking trapped in midtown gridlock, a movie in which Columbus hunts a white whale from sea to shining sea, a TV wrestler about to get punched out by a mad ex-girlfriend, or a book about Levi-Strauss getting used as a door-stop in Jamaica.

Schwarzkopf reached a crescendo, and everything paused—the grand climax! But the words got lost. The words refused their targets, trapped in the general's mouth. Time had been thoroughly traumatized, but refused to go any further, refused to become a souvenir, and Schwarzkopf could only stare at the big blank space that time had forced him to see, stare in fear as the Goodyear blimp crashed into the Statue of Liberty.

The newsman staggered out into Battery Park, collapsed in deep green grass, looking up into the sky like a fake Walt Whitman. The sophomore dropped her flags in the vomit, felt that her teeth were getting darker, felt like a map of Africa drawn by Columbus, or the Congo River filling up with designer jeans, torn condoms, old magazine articles smeared with blood and vaseline, torn blueprints. She staggered out onto the street, thought about changing her major to physics, or quitting and starting her own boutique, or writing scathing social critiques for the *Voice* or *Ms*. magazine. She found herself looking past the blood-smeared clouds and the general's print-smeared face, looking into the gap in time and space, the heart of darkness, dreaming of Marlon Brando as Colonel Kurtz in *Apocalypse Now*, watching the Goodyear blimp descend in flames on Ellis Island.

6/10/91

THE GOTHIC TWILIGHT

It's mid-summer 1990, dense green clouds and the Greenhouse Effect. The President gets an expected call from his friends at Central Intelligence, telling him that Iraq is just about to invade Kuwait. The President's already said that he doesn't care. His ambassador several days ago made it clear that Arab conflicts don't concern the United States, at least not when it's a border dispute. That's considered a regional issue. But now the President's been advised that it might be smart to seem concerned, and to use brute force to make that concern fully evident. The President looks out the window into the Garden of Delights, a knife between two human ears, a face turning into a tree. Let Saddam Hussein assume that his rage with Kuwait won't be interfered with, then act indignant when he invades and call him the Butcher of Baghdad. The report from the Task Force back in the spring spelled everything out quite clearly, that the Middle East was high on the growing list of U.S. priorities, a zone to be controlled, and now the time is ripe for invasion, a perfect way to make America seem like a world police force, and at the same time firmly establish regional domination, making it all seem ethical with rhetoric about human rights, getting the U.N. Security Council prepared to support intervention, setting the stage for talk of a New World Order, something to take people's minds off the fact that America's no longer functioning, except as a place where military force can be manufactured.

The President remembers the plenary meeting back in April, when all the major powers met in the Garden of Delights, a circle of nude white manikins mounted on polymorphic animals, parading in a circle fronting a lake and four huge palaces, each one like a vegetable from an unremembered nightmare, rotting in spots, cut open or punctured or twisted or badly distorted, massive microbiotic forms consuming tiny humans, all displayed in a mild mid-afternoon light, and the goal of the meeting was clear—to make sure France, Japan, Great Britain and Germany knew just what to expect, eliciting their support, or at least a pledge of non-interference. Meanwhile Dole and Baker were telling Hussein to get rid of his weapons, to leave his nation defenseless, while Israel did nothing about its weapons of mass destruction, its hundred nuclear warheads purchased illegally from the White House, its chemical or biological weapons, its ongoing research, and Saddam glared, then laughed and looked away. They had to be kidding. But the President called it diplomacy, and the papers reported that Saddam Hussein was mad, wouldn't listen to reason.

The President gets off the phone. He knows that everything is in place. He'll appear that night with *Amnesty International*'s latest report, statistics on Iraq's human rights violations. He'll claim he's really upset, that the murders and tortures need to be answered, even though in the past he never cared if Hussein was murdering Kurds. Killing them was fine until deploring it fit the U.S. agenda. The President knows how to look really sad and concerned in front of the cameras, the Garden of Delights in the windows in back of him, a polymorphic insect perched on a throne beside a smiling pig, gasping human heads peering out from a drum, hands reaching out from a trumpet, bleeding male and female torsos trapped in the strings of a massive lute, a serpent coiled on the fretboard sinking its fangs into someone's throat.

The President walks up and down in the Oval Office. He tries to clear his throat but his body trembles. He's on the verge of being replaced by everything he resembles. He's like a throne of dirt, or like a bus getting stuck in reverse. He's like a massive black stone fist in the desert. He's like a heat-wave getting used as a metaphor in a rock song. He's like a bird in a cage in a burning building, like a fake bronze gong. He's like the air going bad in the Virgin Islands. The air conditioning makes it feel like winter, or January 1991 to be precise, the fateful day, and time can't wait. It gets cut up and recombined, a cinematic *tour de force*, a jump-cut into Star Wars, just in time for the six o'clock news and a message from the White House. The President wants to describe the world as an optical illusion, even though he has no U.N. permission to bomb Iraq, or do anything but force Iraqi troops to withdraw from Kuwait. But the guns and the TV cameras are all in place, and all attempts at peace have been dismissed as attacks on freedom. The President's face appears on the TV screen to address the nation. Everyone waits, desperate for some fun, for wild sensations. Hi-tech thunder and lightning fill the hi-tech sky above Baghdad. Announcers compare the tension to the Hindenburgh disaster. Then back to the President facing the TV nation from his office, the Garden of Delights in the windows in back of him, Adam and Eve in a giant bubble above a dark red ball, inside of which a face looks out and a big black rat looks back, a blackbird biting a frog at the feet of God near the Tree of Knowledge, which looks like a bright pink rocketship that's crashed in a pool of mirrors. Two huge flocks of birds weave in and out between three spires of rock, forming a double helix carefully cutting and stitching the dense blue sky, beneath which a white rubber elephant stares at a black and blue plastic giraffe.

The President's grave look and firmly practiced mode of address, combined with the carefully scripted CNN footage, make any revealing analysis of his motives highly unlikely, especially when so much of the nation is tired of scandals and crooks in the White House, tired of not indulging in patriotic self-deception. So the question of why it's crucial to get Kuwait's dictator back into power, to protect a quasi-feudal family worth billions, never comes up. It's buried by footage of obsolete battleships blasting Iraq from the Persian Gulf, dramatic pictures of Mighty Mo on newsstands and TV screens, nostalgia for World War II, for pre-Vietnam days of glory. But no one explains what it means for U.S. banks and corporations, that they need to make sure the Al-Sabah family doesn't feel abandoned, that the U.S. economy might well collapse if the family that rules Kuwait withdrew its investments, so from the point of view of corporate America, a viewpoint made to seem like objective truth by the national media, Kuwait's human rights violations don't exist, even though they appear in the latest *Amnesty* report, the same one the President's using to justify his attack on Iraq.

Senator Gonzalez reports that the war is unconstitutional, instituting impeachment proceedings, but nobody cares, and the President smiles. It's a grim smile, to be sure. He knows that a wide grin might seem out of place. But he looks the nation square in the face from the TV screen. He sees everything. He sees that although the fake polls make it seem that the people support him, huge numbers of people are deeply depressed, enraged. They'd like to kill him. The only reason they don't is because it might look bad on their resumés. It would still be considered a crime in the courts, where certain kinds of crime don't pay.

The camera zooms in close. It goes through the President's face, through the President's brain. It zeroes in on the Garden of Delights in the mirror behind him, the torn green light and the dark towns in the background, bubbling pools of blood, a mirror turning into a tree, a rabbit eating the severed legs of a young flamenco dancer. A long procession of nude men marches into the door of a huge blue egg, a man's legs squirm in the grip of a giant clam on a young woman's back. The nation looks at these images for a long time. Then the President speaks: During the Middle Ages, painting was not what it is today. It played a minor role compared with architecture and sculpture, functioning as a decorative art that served the needs of the church. But by the fifteenth century, the Christian view had begun to change. The notion that God was implicit in every element of nature—a romantic idea, to be sure—set the stage for the physical world, in all its manifestations, to serve as a source of religious inspiration. Nature and man were suddenly worth attention, suddenly seen as more than stage machinery, seen as potential sources of truth for the first time since antiquity. And this transformation—spurred as it was by nominalist perspectives, philosophies that turned men away from abstract universals, directing them toward the search for the individual—led painters to develop techniques of accurate reproduction, mirror-like representations of the life they perceived all around them.

There's canned applause in the studio, but the President suddenly seems depressed, like his eyes might turn to stone, his hair might suddenly catch fire. He looks like he's just stepped off a plane, smiling for the cameras, but really grinding his teeth on the verge of panic, having seen a movie on the flight about an airplane crash, after which it became quite clear that a TV can solve its own problems, depriving the future of what it does best, a process that can't be clearly defined because it hasn't occurred yet, a form of leisure best expressed in parallel conversations, two couples in the same supermarket breaking up after fights about sex, rage developing out of precisely the same lame verbal confusions, the same lame verbal conventions, an imprecision dissolving into a doberman breaking in through the door, bounding into the Oval Office, leaping up on the President's desk and messing up all his papers.

More than a hundred thousand people stand outside the White House. They're chanting: No Blood for Oil! Impeach Bush and Quayle! Bring the Troops Home Now! It goes on all day long, and the crowd's much larger the following weekend. Demonstrations occur in major cities all over the nation. But they rate little more than a brief dismissive remark or two on the nightly news, and the reasons millions of people oppose the war don't get much air time.

But lots of time goes into promoting the President's views on Renaissance art. The news teams find his insights really incisive. They especially like his emphasis on "the conquest of the visible world, the need to explore and bring to the canvas a nearly photographic sense of the natural world that surrounds us." They ask the President what he meant. But before he can get to his answer, a big red beak breaks in through the tall French windows in his office. A sequence of sirens begins. The President's limo is covered with insects. It's clear that the President needs to be tuned up. He's not really functioning. But the parts they need to fix him aren't on hand. They'll have to be ordered, and the place where they usually get them has gone out of business.

NEW WORLD ORDER

NEW WORLD ORDER

Just before dawn, Columbus thinks he can see land in the distance, but in the dark of a subway station a man gets pushed and falls on the tracks. The belated screech of the train's brakes quickly becomes a loud guitar solo, the opening of the latest acid rock video, and suddenly there's a ship in a turbulent ocean, lyrics about Columbus finding another world by mistake, and the camera shifts to the singer's face—they've made him up to look vaguely obscene, and he seems to become Jim Morrison, or Columbus, on the deck of a ship, then back to the subway station, back to the man getting pushed on the tracks, except that it's not a man this time but a woman wearing a white lace dress, a juxtaposition of images that seems to make no immediate sense, a strange effect that seems at first quite poetic, except that it isn't designed to present a complex interpretive problem. The video's images go by much too fast for careful thinking. They move in a rhythm designed to control the pace of the viewer's attention, yanking it through a jarring, never-quite-settled rush of impressions, getting the viewer's adrenaline moving, pushing toward an ecstasy that allows no self-awareness, Columbus gazing into the flashing sea of electronic images, cymbals crashing at sunrise, dolphins leaping and splashing, Columbus pumping his bass while frothing waves turn into the White House, where a George Bush look-alike tries to look really mean as he pounds on his drum kit, mermaids leaping, splashing in widening circles, then a hurricane, Columbus pacing the deck unable to find the magic symbols, the incantation that might bring the storm to an end, a long guitar solo, then Columbus comes back with his bass and his piercing vocals, lyrical ironies, referring to Christian hypocrisy and the slave trade, all the gold in Cathay, but somehow Columbus remains charismatic, made-up to look really sexy, to sell the group's mass image, to make the record company rich, even as the words of the song refer to concentration camps, Columbus taking a Taino Indian princess onto his flagship, holding her three days and nights in his cabin, savage drumbeat, footage of sexual violence interspersed with a subway disaster, the singer's face coming out of the shadows, mermaids trapped in strobe light, tortured guitar improvisations, grinding wheels in the darkness.

But later Jimmy, the group's producer, feels that the video needs to be changed. There's got to be more sex. They need more close-ups of Columbus. The parts about President Bush might need to be clarified or deleted. And he's not sure at all that the subway scene really works, or the circle of mermaids. He knows that Richard wants the song he wrote represented clearly, a pop critique of Eurocaucasian arrogance. But he also knows that the video's got to make money, that political statements are fine so long as they don't reduce the group's mass appeal, so long as the lyrics don't call too much attention to themselves, don't interfere with the mesmerizing rhythm of visual images. Richard likes the connection between Columbus and the White House, the way it links two systems of oppression. But he can't be sure if the video's visual thrust is completely appropriate. It's fun to look sexy on stage, and Richard really knows how to look sexy. In the case of this song, however, Richard's not sure that a macho image makes sense. If the image sells the song, then lots of people get the message. But he knows that the selling techniques are part of the message.

He thinks of Columbus near the Cape of the Star in western Haiti*, writing in his journal about his nights with the captive princess, claiming that she wanted him so much that she wouldn't go back to her tribe, leaving out the fact that she'd been tied to his bed and repeatedly forced, that when she finally got free she quickly jumped overboard with an anchor, sinking to the bottom of the sea, disappearing forever, but soon Richard's back in the studio pumping his bass and looking sexy, iridescent blue-green lighting

---

*The native American tribes in the Caribbean referred to Haiti as Bohío; the Spaniards called it Hispañiola. The modern name is used here to make the location easier to visualize for the modern reader. Modern names have also been used with most of the other islands.

making the stage look vaguely aquatic, as if the band were jamming at the bottom of the sea, windows in the waves and light coming in like spoiled asparagus. The focus blurs and soon we're in the dim light of a subway platform. A woman wearing a wedding dress gets pushed on the tracks by the band's lead guitarist, who whirls back facing the camera, tries to look insane, blurred focus, a shift, Columbus walking back and forth gazing into the darkness, watching a light that's like a tiny wax candle rising and falling. We're supposed to believe, like Columbus himself, that the light's on the coast of China, that the morning will soon reveal the ports of the Great Khan blazing with silver and gold. But the morning shows nothing but ocean rising and falling.

The lyrics refer to the fact that Columbus had offered a big reward, that the first man to see land would get the gold coin Columbus had nailed to a mast. But Columbus claims the reward for himself, even though the land wasn't there, even though the false alarms cost many men a good night's sleep. The ocean turns into the White House, the George Bush look-alike looking demented and pounding his drums in the blue room, dissolving back to the blue-green quasi-aquatic stage in the studio. Everything's in a groove and the band's really moving. But outside the studio things aren't quite so removed.

The noisy light of Columbus Circle makes Richard feel suicidal, and he feels even worse when he looks up at the statue of Columbus. The Admiral stares downtown with chiseled eyes and lips and hands on hips, his look suggesting the title of Richard's song, "The New World Order," the Gulf & Western Building rising a thousand feet behind his head, his thick hair covered with dirt and dry white bird-shit. Richard feels like he needs cocaine—or as he tells himself, he *wants* cocaine; he doesn't *need* it. But the city looks out of place, like it's all behind a huge glass door, which might not be so bad, except that the glass is cracked, discolored. He thinks that Columbus's head is like a room completely made of doors, fake doors opening out on cardboard skies and plastic oceans. At times he can hear a fake knock and someone starts to come in, looks up and down, can't quite figure out where he or she is, and goes back out, as if there were some kind of endless complaint in his head, or fake wood paneling.

Richard knows that people who complain all the time are

boring, that people who don't complain at all are boring, that Columbus imagines a gong each time he comes up with a name for an island. Richard's situation might be described as a feast of comparison, a dark-feathered crane with a mirror in place of its head, stars reflected at noon, a woman's voice proclaiming doom in a city of islands at midnight, a bolt of lightning dropping out of clear blue skies, a tradition of lies, a fire that won't go out on the Persian Gulf, a burning cross in Iraq, a lunar eclipse in Jamaica made to look like an act of magic, a cartoon bear skating toward a huge crack on a pond of ice in a beer commercial, a cold wind making water boil near a volleyball game in Cuba. Richard begins to feel like a mouse in a maze, like someone who rips pay telephones down coming home from work each night, like someone whose body's been torn apart and left on a thousand islands.

Richard thinks of going home, but his wife won't let him back in. He married a female body-building champion two years ago, but once the initial chemistry had worn off there was open warfare. Soon she was physically beating him up each time they had a bad fight, feeling horrible afterwards, apologizing profusely, yet feeling that Richard was somehow baiting her into losing control. The therapist they finally consulted came up with "a radical remedy," advising them to act their conflicts out in S&M clubs, playing the roles that turned them on until the roles became boring. But getting dressed up and acting out scenes in the clubs only made things worse. Their fights at home intensified, and Richard soon decided he'd better get out, moving in with Bob, the group's new drummer, a guy whose chief claim to fame was that he looked just like George Bush, a guy that Charlotte suspected of being gay and seducing her husband, even though Bob had many times made blunt homophobic statements.

Several years before, Charlotte had gone through a series of traumas, painful and sudden shifts in what she felt and how she acted, leaving her in the grip of at least three secret personalities. To make her host personality strong enough to control the others, she's developed a big and muscular physique. She excels in athletics. But behind this outwardly powerful projection, she thinks of herself as a number of different people—all of whom become dominant from time to time and express themselves.

At first, she'd made up names for all her different secret

identities. It gave her a means of keeping track of who they were and what they did. Later, consulting a hypnotist, she remembered some of her previous lives, and even though she couldn't quite get the names of all the people she'd been, she saw where some of her sub-personalities came from. And without really making his true identity known, one of these people seems to be Columbus.

When Charlotte's at the gym, Columbus looks for signs of an oncoming gale. The sky looks utterly placid, not a cloud in sight, no change in the wind. But it's in the motion of waves that Columbus makes all his weather predictions. Columbus thinks he can read the motion of chaos, that the absent center of the ocean sea is the missing phallus of Europe. His ears begin to bite their way toward his brain, but his brain's already become hot food in the teeth of his inward gaze. The language in the Admiral's head begins to seem unrealistic.

There's been quick sailing for nearly a month, but Columbus wakes on September 10th in a place that's filled with rumors, in miles of dense green seaweed someone later calls the Sargasso Sea, a sea inside a sea, slowly circling into a spiral, as if the entire site were a massive octopus dead from pollution, a sea where moonlight's trapped in a maze of waving blue-green algae, a microbiotic structure made of the world's first living things, now becoming five hundred miles of a question curling up into itself, a sea like a letter C curving into a circle, a huge copyright sign, a black hole sucking in garbage as if by design from every direction, and soon they reach the horse latitudes, where the weather becomes bad grammar, where a fist comes up from the flat sea stopping all motion, stopping all sound and speech, and the deck turns into a matchbox, and the wind can't move, can't find its own feet. The water becomes white brick and the sunlight's black like an over-cooked hot dog. The future stops, turns back like a traumatized watch dog. This is the point where the words become realistic, as if certain years had been stashed away somewhere and acquired a new function, no longer parts of a temporal sequence trapped in past and future.

Columbus doesn't lose his mind. He knows where it is at all times. He keeps it locked in a little white box in his bedroom when he sleeps, and when he's awake on deck it's on a short leash and feigns obedience. But the problem is that he can't understand how it works, how it makes its own motion, which might be described in mechanistic terms, a kind of conveyor belt, where the product conveyed is a careful description of how the belt itself was made, but since Columbus doesn't know what a conveyor belt is he remains in the dark, a state of mind that could also be described in mechanistic terms, but again these terms would make no sense to Columbus, would leave him in a dense linguistic darkness, would complicate the fact that the maps he's made behave like mirrors, making Cathay look like a big turnip, making it seem perhaps three thousand miles due east of its true location, a miscalculation made even worse by the fact that Columbus falsifies the distances they've traveled, repeatedly telling his men—who don't have time to pay too much attention—that they've sailed perhaps one hundred miles beyond their true position, or using the phrase "We're not far from here" when their questions become too persistent.

Soon Columbus gets confused by his own misleading statements. He begins to get lost in the world that he's constructed for himself, and when the physical world breaks in, it feels like a major disaster. His powers of discernment fade. He can't tell the difference between a black and white cube and a game of chance, or between a brick chimney collapsing, struck by lightning, and a phrase that makes it seem that the morning sky is a massive eggshell, or between a heliocentric notion of space and a fake mountain waterfall, or between a description of rain and fear disguised as a theory of motion, between a baby throwing food at breakfast and a house of black bones, between a ship on stage and a pig in a pen, its throat getting cut before dawn, between a chair getting chopped up, used as firewood, and a sequence of concentric circles trapped in a schoolboy's head, or between the Fountain of Youth and the Book of the Dead.

The space in front of the Admiral's cold face heats up like a skillet, becoming so non-adhesive nothing holds in place, begins to slide, vanishing into the sea, leaving what looks like a convex mirror. But what it seems to reflect doesn't look very much like the Admiral's face, doesn't look like anything else, and doesn't even look like itself. Columbus feels like someone who's gotten fat again after ten thin years, like someone who's just about to get used in a sandwich, and he hears what sounds like a mouth filling up with fried eggs two feet behind him, or the sound of a mouth wired shut as a dieting strategy.

The veins in Charlotte's arms look really pumped up in the

health club mirrors. From several different angles, she can watch her biceps bulge. It's part of a whole new concept of feminine glamor, and though it appeared at first to be part of women's liberation, it now seems little more than the latest mass commodity fashion, a way to get people to buy a new mode of packaging their bodies. Or at least that's what she imagines Richard would say at the start of an argument, a fight that might get physical if he said the wrong things too many times. Charlotte knows that her anger's out of proportion, that a lot of it's aimed at her father for molesting her as a child. But psychotherapeutic formulas don't mean much when the fighting begins, and Charlotte's glad he's gone. She thinks her life's more sane without him, especially since Columbus wants more time as her demon lover, especially since Columbus was born with a fork stuck into the bridge of his nose, especially since he's about to find out that fleas can't survive in the Indies.

Lost in the night, he decides to follow great flocks of birds, changing his course, turning away from the Gulf Stream sailing south in a mild and fragrant breeze. All night long, Columbus and his crew can hear dark wingbeats, and at times they can even see silhouettes of wings against the moon. Time becomes obsolete but motion remains, a late-night walk in the rain, a dog waking up on top of a washing machine, a burning weathervane. It's 2 a.m., October 12, and someone sees a white cliff trapped in moonlight, and then there's another white cliff, and a line of dark sand running between them. It's all maybe six miles away, and it holds in place. It's not an illusion. It's given the name San Salvador, and soon the flags of Aragon and Castille are unfurled on the sandy shore, Columbus greeting the Tainos with bright glass beads and big white smile, noting how friendly they seem, noting how well their flesh is proportioned, noting they're not ashamed without anything on, that they're not speaking Spanish. Everything looks lovely—the trees really seem to know how to be green—but he knows that he's not in Cathay, that the Queen doesn't care about beautiful scenery.

Richard thinks that as an ironic touch they should use travel posters, making the big discovery look like a tourist guidebook image, then juxtaposing footage of the U.S. invading Grenada, with Bob made up to look like President Bush sitting in on bongos, then a jump-cut to the shanty towns on the southern coast of Barbados.

Jimmy likes the part about Bush on bongos, but he thinks the rest is a bit clichéd, and besides, his boss won't buy it. If you're going to make statements, Jimmy says, be clever, don't overdo it. People don't turn on M-TV to get preached at.

Richard often thinks that it might be better to make his own videos, sink his capital into making something he really believes in. But he knows that with no distribution what he wants to say won't reach anyone, that the corporations alone permit him to speak and sing to the nation. He sits in the penthouse apartment he shares with Bob and broods, looking out at the clouds, thinking that each might one day bear the flag of United Airlines, the Friendly Skies, a copyright sign coming up on the sun each morning.

Jimmy thinks that "The New World Order" is just a phase that Richard's in, that he falls into peevish moods from time to time and gets moralistic. Two years before, for instance, Richard wrote a piece for *Rolling Stone*, a scathing critique of the corporate scum that control the music business, naming names and providing very careful documentation. But no one seemed to get too upset. Sales weren't hurt in the slightest. Richard's records and videos sold even better after the essay appeared. The company's top executives openly joked with Richard about his rage, but Jimmy's afraid that they won't be pleased if the product itself reveals too much, if it rocks the boat, especially if the man getting trashed is an admiral.

Columbus will soon be the Dean of Pain, Admiral of the Ocean Sea. He imagines anchoring off the coast of Cathay, dispatching an envoy, entrusting him with all due diplomatic paraphrenalia: a passport in Latin, a letter of credence in Latin from Queen Isabella, and most important a person to translate from Latin and Spanish into Chinese. Even though this person has never spoken Chinese, he's pressed into service; after all, he's had conversations with African kings—they're almost Chinese.

Columbus imagines meeting the Great Khan himself in a marvelous chamber, filled with gold and courtiers and strange but lovely music, showing him the letter from the Queen, which in translation reads: I'm here to take possession of all your wealth and land, your labor force, to change what you believe and how you educate your children. Columbus imagines the scene with great satisfaction. The Great Khan blinks in amazement, searching the Admiral's face for signs of a joke, but finding none he looks down

NEW WORLD ORDER

and clears his throat, turns toward his advisors, who simply shrug and look away, embarrassed or confused. So the Great Khan stares at his feet and finally says: Ummm...Yeah, sure, no problem. The kingdom's all yours. We're sure you'll enjoy it. Columbus grins and shakes the Great Khan's hand. He looks like a baseball star, smiling for the cameras after stealing home in the last of the ninth, winning the final game of a hotly contested World Series.

But the Tainos never mention Cathay, the Great Khan or his kingdom. As far as Columbus can tell from a very crude process of translation, the Tainos don't care about gold or kings. They don't have political struggles. They like the trinkets Columbus brings because they're brightly colored. But they don't have the same frame of reference at all about money and power, feeling and action. The only thing Columbus comes away sure of is that they're not alone, that Salvador is one of a thousand islands, and that one of those islands contains a tribe of amazons, women whose physical strength has made them a legend. Even the Carib tribe from the southern coast of Crooked Island—a tribe the Tainos describe as fierce, a tribe described as a band of practicing cannibals by Columbus—won't go anywhere near the amazon island, Martinino, which seems to be off the Cape of the Star near the northwest coast of Haiti. Columbus thinks it might be fun to make those amazons Christian, to sell them back in Spain as domestic servants, saving for the circus those that won't be tamed or converted, so before he leaves he gets the Tainos to steer him toward the Cape of the Star, even though he's not at all sure that he's understood their language.

But language isn't meant to be understood, it's meant to be spoken. Or at least that's what Columbus tells himself when he writes in his journal. The self is what you tell yourself it is, Columbus tells himself, and Charlotte agrees, changing herself with each mirrored repetition, watching her powerful arms, each muscle big with definition. Last year she won the Ms. Olympia contest. This year she'd like to be the new Ms. Galaxy. And she's pretty sure that she will, now that Richard's not there to make trouble.

She thought it was pretty exciting at first, beating him in playful wrestling matches. But when it got nasty, she started to feel really strange. The radical sex club remedy, the acted scenes of muscle and submission, had seemed to be working at first, but soon the fighting at home came back, focused on some kind of conflict that

THE GOTHIC TWILIGHT

never quite got resolved. Charlotte had wanted to go back into therapy, but Richard thought they'd just be wasting money, that since they got a big thrill from their physical fights, they weren't about to give up what was giving them such pleasure, that the fights were a means of keeping away from deeper forms of disturbance. The only way to get sane was separation.

Richard sits in front of M-TV at four in the morning, watching yet another narcissistic male performer, dancing in front of adoring teenage girls on a flashing stage, looking nonchalant, then torn with rage, then wild with passion, modeling his face and the latest fashion. Richard knows that billions of dollars go into producing trash like this, promotional drivel that high-brow culture critics like to write articles on, pointing out all the subtle ironic references that the video makes, parodies of the gestures and facial expressions of Cold War film stars, deflating its own seductive appeal but still enticing millions. Richard himself has many times made videos just like this. Indeed, his reputation is to some extent based on such videos. And if his producer prevails "The New World Order" will quickly become yet another mass media sensation, teenage girls going wild with Columbus on bass and Bush on bongos, fires in the Persian Gulf and seagulls covered with oil, surf like tar, Baghdad collapsing in flames on M-TV, a bride getting pushed on the tracks, screech of the train's brakes quickly becoming a double-tracked guitar solo, Columbus peering into the sun with mirror shades and a fake white beard, blue designer tank top showing off his tanning salon physique, Richard having spent long weeks working out with his wife to look toned and strong, Columbus fighting a sequence of very stiff trade winds looking for amazons.

But he also keeps thinking that maybe there aren't any amazons, that maybe the Tainos meant something else, and besides, what good are amazons to the Queen? She sent him out to find gold. He's pretty sure that she wouldn't be much impressed with Christianized amazons. Still he pushes on. He's got to find out why the Tainos were terrified, why merely mentioning Martinino Island made them uneasy, drove them into a frenzy, if indeed that's what it was, if indeed he's reading their body language with any precision. He thinks he can recognize fear when he sees it, that certain emotions don't get lost in translation, that comprehending certain reactions doesn't depend on context.

NEW WORLD ORDER

But the captain of the *Pinta*, Martín Alonso Pinzón, is pretty sure that the Tainos aren't what Columbus thinks they are. He's not convinced at all that they're noble savages, that all they need is a little Christianization. He thinks they're setting Columbus up, that they secretly work for the Great Khan and they're pointing him into the teeth of a storm, steering him away from the golden spires and domes of the mystical East. This thought occurs to Columbus too, but he can't quite believe that he's getting conned. His thoughts get all messed up, get badly tangled in the trade winds. The words that hold his mind in place go off in a thousand directions. So Columbus imagines a magnet, and the words get pulled back in. Now it's merely a matter of moving them into the proper sequence, which gets a bit confusing, since Columbus himself is a word that's part of the sequence, and he's not sure where his name belongs, or whether he ought to refer to himself as I or he or Columbus.

But one thing does seem clear: he can't find gold, he really feels anxious. He knows that he's got to show the Queen something tangible besides parrots and fruits. For three straight nights he gets bad dreams about disappointing his mother. But then he thinks of the Portuguese, their brave new African enterprise, and a light goes on, dollar signs on parade behind his eyes: The Tainos might make perfect slaves. They seem so nice and passive. He sends his toughest man, Alonso Hojeda, on shore to find some. Hojeda soon gets a Taino chief to wear handcuffs, claiming they're bracelets, royal gifts from the great white gods in the land beyond the sunrise. The chief goes mad, gnaws at his chains in jail, destroys all his teeth, cracking his skull while frantically trying to bash his head through the prison walls. Soon Hojeda tricks other chiefs into chains, begins a triumphant march, turning the land from paradise into a massive colonial death camp.

At one point Hojeda's men follow rhythmic drumming into the jungle, tracing it back to a Taino celebration, where men and women dance in complex patterns in the moonlight. The Spaniards rush in, brandishing swords, hacking off the drummers' arms, watching them bleed and then slicing off their heads and rolling them over the ground. Then they attack the dancers, cutting open their bellies, knocking their entrails out on the ground and splitting their heads wide open. Those that try to escape find their legs tangled up in their own intestines. Everywhere there's bursting blood and screaming. No one survives. Events like this take place all over Haiti every day, a way to convince the Tainos that white men don't play games.

Later the Tribute System begins. Despite the fact that there isn't much gold, Taino males over fourteen years of age are given quotas, required to furnish four hawkbells full of gold dust every month. The alternative is death, and some try to run off into the mountains. They're hunted down with dogs. Many get sliced up, used as trophies. Others are tortured and forced to return, and thousands take their own lives instead of becoming slaves in gold mines, breaking their backs and learning Christian platitudes in Latin.

Richard wants the emphasis put on colonial destruction. But Jimmy's making the video, and he knows what the company wants: something in line with the quincentenial jubilees, the hundred million dollars getting spent on Columbus festivities, the pseudo-patriotic celebrations all over the hemisphere. Jimmy thinks there's already been quite enough Columbus bashing. He's tired of people like Richard complaining, tired of all the revisionistic seminars, the films and books, making Columbus look like a Renaissance Hitler, connecting him with President Bush and his desert conflagration. He thinks what America needs right now is to feel its strength as a nation. But somewhere deep inside he knows the facts can't be denied, that the violence of Richard's critique is totally justified, and besides, the violent images might help sell the product, especially if they're accompanied by shots of Richard's hot physique, his moody eyes and long blond hair and photogenic cheekbones.

Columbus feels like a notebook left in a bathroom in a burning house, a whirlpool stained with the blood of a horse thrown overboard and thrashing, a bag of trash getting used as crucial evidence in a murder case, a roach on a dead man's face, a cub scout master framed as a rapist. His cabin spins on the deck. The ship's in the grip of dark enchantments, of storms whose violence only becomes apparent three days after the fact, assuming words like *fact* make any sense in such a context. Words get bent out of shape, distort any brain that tries to repeat them, distort what they describe, distort the system they comprise.

Columbus can't turn back. He's trapped in the storm of Charlotte's body. He's looking out from her eyes at the muscle she's pumping up in the mirror. She doesn't really know that she's

Columbus. She only knows that part of her seems gone, part of her's moving away, another part's coming back. But they don't have names, and they don't seem friendly. Charlotte goes to meetings every Tuesday night at the church on her block, where she and other multiples trade stories about their condition. Some of the others have had themselves hypnotized too. They've learned who the people inside them probably are, or at least who they claim to be, and it's odd that they always seem to be famous people. But Charlotte can't afford to be too skeptical. She needs the support. She needs to find out what's going on before it begins to affect her career. She knows that people all over the country think of her as a goddess. What would they think if they knew she was three different people?

At a recent meeting someone told Charlotte he thought she might be Jim Morrison, that he thought she'd been possessed by Morrison's ghost, and though she'd always thought spirit possession was just another word for psychosis, in this case what the man was proposing didn't seem out of the question. Indeed, it was quite consistent with how she felt in the Columbus mode, even though she'd always thought that Morrison was a jerk. She would have preferred being told that she'd been inhabited by John Lennon, but Lennon's nice guy genius public image had no connection at all with how she thought and felt when Columbus took over.

Columbus thinks that before he dies, he wants to hear a butterfly scream, and he wants to hear lots of other things too, like Beatriz de Peraza's voice on the pillow beside him in bed, the billowing drapes and the sound of waves through the open window beside them. He'd stopped on the Grand Canary for wood and food and other necessities, but gotten delayed by the island's owner, Beatriz. Columbus at first wasn't clear that having sex with her made sense. After all, his wife back in Spain was called Beatriz too; it might get him confused. But Beatriz de Peraza quickly convinced him. Her brassy aggressive manner was just what he'd always been afraid to want, just what he'd always imagined when he played with himself in the bathroom, having settled in marriage for someone less arrogant, less overtly perverse. Beatriz de Peraza knew how to play the dominatrix, and then how to play the nurturing mother once the hot passion was over. Columbus fit her fantasies completely. On the level of wit, on the level of learning and social sophistication,

Columbus was clearly beneath her. She played with him like a female science professor seducing a student. His wild ambition seemed wonderfully quaint, and yet he clearly knew how to get things done, how to be convincing, especially in bed. After all, she thought, he'd gotten his way with the Queen. Hundreds of others had come with less absurd and costly proposals. But Columbus had been a master at coping with bureaucratic abuse, and after eight years of red tape and careful appearances in the Queen's boudoir, Columbus had come away with a highly seductive business arrangement. Assuming he found Cathay, he'd soon be Admiral of the Ocean Sea, and Beatriz found this cumbersome overblown title weirdly sexy. Besides, her name was perfect: Every Dante needs a Beatrice, even if her inspiration wasn't quite pure, not even romantic, even if it might have been slightly sado-masochistic.

Columbus dreams of Beatriz every night, thinks he can see her face in the tropical stars from his cabin window, working his way through the pulsing dark in search of the island of amazons. Hojeda tries to remind Columbus of gold and slaves and the ports of Cathay, but Columbus feels like a madman searching the seas to kill a white whale. He's not in control but he knows how to get what he wants, or what he thinks he wants. He knows how to track his obsessions, knocking everything out of his way.

But early on the morning of December 25th, maybe three hours before dawn, a cloudy moonless night, Columbus makes a big mistake. He lets Hojeda go to sleep early, leaving an inexperienced young man on deck to steer the ship, someone who's never tried to stay up all night and soon goes to sleep on his feet. Suddenly, the *Santa Maria* crashes into a coral reef, nearly splitting in half, sinking quickly. It's all Columbus can do to save himself and most of his crew. They drag themselves up on shore near Cape Haitien at 5 a.m., falling asleep in the sand completely traumatized and exhausted. The other two ships work day and night to salvage the wood from the wreckage, and the wood gets used on the shore to build a fortress, the first official port of the New World Order.

Richard finds the whole thing really amusing—the name of the ship, the fact that it got wrecked on Christmas morning, that from its resurrected frame a brand new world and mythos came, and Richard wants the new video to include a symbolic shipwreck. On this point he and Jimmy agree. Superimposed on the scene with

Bush and Columbus drumming and smiling, there's footage of *The Pequod* spinning and sinking, the very stirring scene at the end of the movie *Moby Dick*, the ravings of Gregory Peck as Ahab having dissolved in rising foam, right before the final somber words of Richard Basehart. Jimmy and Richard aren't at all disturbed that the image is borrowed, that older viewers may well remember the movie and make the connection. Jimmy knows that similar techniques work for Madison Avenue, and Richard likes the connection of Columbus and Captain Ahab—after all, both men were torn with masochistic passion, the very same passion that Richard now sees in himself and tries to steer clear of.

But part of him goes to sleep at times, and soon he's on the phone, he's dialing pain, he wants to see Charlotte.

He says: Hi, honey. Howya doing. It's me.

And she says, after a pause: Oh hi Richard. I'm OK, how are you?

He says: Not bad, but I could be better. What are you doing tonight?

She hesitates: Tonight? Well, I've got some plans...I'm meeting my friend Beatrice. We're going—

But Richard says: Who's Beatrice?

She starts to lie but stops herself. She summons all her strength and says: Look Richard, you know I love you. You know there's no one else. But if we got together we'd just be running all the same numbers on each other again, and feeling like shit the next day, and I don't want that, and I don't think you do either.

Richard says: But honey, I'm horny!

Charlotte says: I'm horny too, damnit! But I really need more time for myself right now. Getting together with you is too confusing.

Richard says: Yeah, I know but—

Charlotte cuts him off: Besides, I'm still pretty angry. I'm still pretty raw from when you left. I couldn't process what happened at first. But now I think you were right. And it's giving me time to sort things—

Richard hangs up in disgust. He should have known she'd be hard boiled. She always got satisfaction out of withholding herself—it came easy—using words like *integrity* to conceal her need to be distant. He feels like he wants to bite his way out of his mouth, or like he's about to get folded up and stuffed in a thin white box. Soon the consolation he gets from telling himself that she's totally wrong fades out. He wants cocaine. But he keeps himself under control, pops a few sleeping pills instead. Soon he's dozing off as one of his videos plays on M-TV. Colors and flashing lights move side-to-side on his closing eyelids, bouncing off his brow and moving the room in several directions, like oceans filling up with bleeding whales, massive amounts of money getting spent producing junkmail, dope getting stored in the genitals of a young boy's fake dalmatian, Columbus taking the name of a twentieth-century corporation, Columbus deciding he must be near Nova Scotia, near Greenland, Columbus getting sodomized as a child in the slums of Genoa.

The Tainos help the Spaniards build their fortress. Their leader, Canabo, repeatedly tries to console a sullen Columbus, giving him all the food he needs, showing him where to find water. Columbus leaves thirty men from the *Santa María*, then takes off again, desperate to find gold or the Khan or the amazons, whichever comes first. Pinzón's already gone. He's taken the *Pinta* north to find prisoners. He knows they'll need to have slaves or the Queen just might feel really cheated—all that money invested and nothing to show for it! But Columbus in the *Niña* circles back toward northern Haiti, gritting his teeth and working hard to look tough at times, and then haunted.

Columbus knows that looking right is crucial. He knew that he had to look firm but also flexible in front of the Queen, so he worked with mirrors each day, making sure he could do the right face. With his crew it's the same, and especially now that his flagship's gone. He can't look down. He's got to seem unshaken, but also driven, obsessed, phantasmic, like someone who can speak to the dead, like someone who really needs to. It works pretty well. Hojeda's the only one who's not afraid of him.

Seven years later, Hojeda will make a voyage of his own, claiming to be the first European to go beyond the Indies, to set foot on the continent, accompanied by Amerigo Vespucci, whose book on the voyage will later lead the Medicis to frame his name, using the word America, not Columbia. Vespucci said his trip took place two years before it really did, more than a year before Columbus came to Venezuela. He carefully kept Hojeda's name out of his book, letting his readers think that he himself was in charge of the voyage, yet making Columbus on his deathbed think he was

NEW WORLD ORDER

working to save his name, all the while developing new connections, winning the gradual confidence of the Queen and her favorite courtier, the Admiral's own son, an apparently tragic end to the great man's life. But Richard again finds the whole thing rather amusing: Columbus, who did so well in selling himself, now getting out-sold.

And Jimmy says: You know, I don't think you're being fair. Not everyone who manipulates to get what he wants is a total shit-head. If you yourself hadn't worked really hard to meet the right people—

But Richard says: That's beside the point. The irony's still there, whether it's aimed at me or Columbus. And no, not everyone who plays games to get what he wants is a total shit-head. But there's always going to be someone who can play the game a bit better, someone who—

Jimmy cuts in: Why call it a game? Why not say that it's just the way people operate. They tend to do favors for people they know. And the ones who happen to be in the right place at the right—

Richard can't stand conversations like this. He always gets out-reasoned, even when he begins with a very strong feeling about what he's thinking. No matter how much he's thought things out beforehand, when an argument comes up he tends to feel stupid, and he also tends to assume that the person he's arguing with doesn't feel insecure, that he likes nothing more than an argument he can demolish. Richard wants cocaine again, but he's promised himself and Charlotte that he won't get high for at least a month, a promise he presently feels completely oppressed by.

To make matters worse, tomorrow's the 4th of July, and he hasn't planned anything. Richard tends to think holidays are a nuisance. He finds it oppressive to celebrate things that he can't bring himself to believe in, to see so many people getting worked up over things he finds boring. He's really dreading the 4th because he can't stand all the pointless noise—most Americans seem to feel that noise is patriotic. Charlotte once told Richard that such an attitude was elitist, that most people felt a strong need for a sense of community, that Richard was posing, pretending his needs were somehow more exalted, pretending that he'd gone beyond the common man he secretly was, the common man that his father had been, even if she'd agreed that words like *common* had no meaning.

When Charlotte got worked up over things like this Richard

always got nasty, telling her things that he often thought but normally would have left unsaid. He would tell her that her need to be constantly talking about her emotions, her need to carefully chart out what she felt, was really boring, a leisure-class indulgence, despite her claim that to be a completely liberated woman, to be free of the patriarchal demand that women ought to be seen but not heard, she needed to say what she felt and to say it with feeling. Perhaps it was this more than anything else that made Richard want to go off on his own, perhaps all the psycho-sexual talk was bullshit—or at least that's what she told him when he left, and he felt that she might have been right, even though at the time he said she was out of touch with her own deep guilt, her unresolved and thoroughly over-dramatized rage at her father.

How else could you explain her desire to have big arms and shoulders, to get so strong she could beat most men in contact sports or street fights? How else could you explain that she had a black belt in karate? But in his better moments he knew these questions weren't worth dog-shit, that they came from a desire to explain things away, to get rid of his feelings, to sail off into an oversimplified chaos, the very same chaos that seemed to be on TV ninety-nine percent of the time, making reality seem like a sanctioned gang rape, or someone forgetting to go to his best friend's wedding, someone getting an arm cut off in a place where they make scotch tape, or street noise drowning out a long-delayed and crucial confession, a barker at a circus getting trapped in a long digression, U.S. dollars keeping a tyrant in power in Santo Domingo, an archaeology textbook propping open a stained glass window.

Columbus imagines a room of stained glass windows, erected on the beach at the site of the *Santa María* disaster. But things aren't going well in the fortress at all. The men refuse to behave themselves. They go out looking for women, cutting their way through the dense green jungle, reaching a Taino village. When the women fight they get raped. Their men get shot, and the place gets leveled. Soon there's nothing left. The women are carried back to the fortress, where the Spaniards use them as prostitutes and dancers for a month or two, a wild and festive time that ends with their suicides.

Richard wants their suicides in the video, to show them stabbing themselves and then to show footage from x-rated movies. He thinks of Gulf War pilots being shown porno films before taking off, and he wants to show that exploitation of women has been with us right from the start, that even if Columbus thought of himself as a highly righteous man, he was also a man of his time. He would have burned women as witches and felt no remorse, or thought of torture for sin as a matter of course. Richard imagines Columbus using Agent Orange in the Indies, mining fields of corn, funding research for germ warfare. He's read that Columbus can't be held accountable for what his men did, that things got out of hand and Columbus had no choice, that he felt ashamed, that it's really Pinzón or Hojeda that ought to be blamed. But Richard's not concerned about blame, or at least he's not in this case. The voyage was made in the Admiral's name, a name that's become symbolic, and Richard's more concerned with changing what that symbol means, or doing away with symbols altogether.

Columbus wants to blame all complications on the weather. Lightning splits the morning sky into broken bits of eggshell. Thunder puts the pieces back in place, though some of them don't quite fit, and some get swept up into the sky by a sudden fierce north wind. Speech hangs over Columbus's head in a small balloon that points toward his mouth, indicating what he says. But the north wind can't be stopped. It blows the balloon up into the clouds, and Columbus stands on deck with his mouth wide open but nothing to say. Soon the wind calms down. The word-balloon drops and pops, impaled on a mast. The words crash down like broken glass on the deck. They're bright and cutting, and no one dares to sweep them up or speak another sentence.

The darkening gray sky flashes, pressing in from all directions. It's close, but it's also distant, a turbulent flat backdrop, a monochromatic panel filled with bullet holes, cracked windows, tilting up and down, torn with incoherent voices. When Columbus prays what he says keeps turning into noise that he can't comprehend, but which might be described as two black limousines colliding, having been speeding up and down a mountain road in the dead of night, the drivers driven mad by Haitian starlight.

In one of Richard's first videos two black limousines collided, an image of ruling elites, the USA and the Soviet Union, though in the video nothing was explained. Its meaning was private, and Jimmy jokes with Richard that the image would now need major revision, that one of the limos would have to run out of gas before the collision, the other one spinning off the road, crashing into a palm tree, then subtly recomposed in a flashing sea of digital imagery, footage of the Doors performing "Horse Latitudes" at the Filmore East, Columbus watching a white horse thrash in the sea, mute nostril agony.

Columbus can't figure out how to use the new tools of navigation, so he's forced to rely on dead reckoning, calculating by sight, estimating time and distance, keeping track by starlight. The strain of having to do this day and night soon gets to Columbus. He becomes rather tense, nasty at times, and by the end explosive. If you dropped him out of a plane you could blow up a city. But Columbus can't admit that he's feeling shitty. He glares at the waves all day—everywhere motion, everywhere patterns of light. Yet the typical water molecule moves only four feet during its lifetime. As thoughts like these proliferate, Columbus begins to feel strange. He's forced to see the obvious, that things don't stay the same. When a system is set in motion, initial conditions change. The point of departure only comes into view after things have developed, appearing to be where things began even though it appears much later, veering off right before it begins to make sense, like someone going to jail for pulling teeth without a license, or the moon collapsing into a pile of birds in a room filled with incense.

Columbus knows that if he dreams of little pigs it means good luck, but if he dreams of big pigs it can only mean bad luck, and if he dreams of asparagus on a black plate it means no sex, but if it's on a white plate it means compulsive sex, which need not be confused with really good sex or even passion, though it may suggest a kind of unending lust in a frigid climate, and if he dreams that he's up to his neck in mud it means that he needs a new name, and if there's a frog in the mud it means that he'll get one, and if he dreams of blackbirds making figure-eights in the twilight, it means that a really strange man will soon appear on deck without warning, becoming friends with everyone but Columbus, and if he dreams of breakfast in a small café at sunrise, it means that all the maps in the world were drawn by bad musicians, and if he dreams of a white mouse in a confession booth near Paris, it means that he'll soon be embarrassed by one of his friends on a solemn occasion, and if he dreams of a dead tree standing tall and white in a fresh green field, it means that he'll soon be making a speech on a subject that can't be determined, and if he dreams of a turbulent silver sky above Toledo, it means that America's nothing more than a painting by El Greco. But Columbus never dreams. He doesn't like to. He'd rather go to sleep in a room that's always filled with bright balloons, and Richard thinks they should pop a water balloon to begin the new video.

Jimmy thinks that Richard's missing the point, that his need to seem politically correct has narrowed his vision. Jimmy wants the video focused on struggle and exploration, making the voyage out to be a metaphor of discovery, of finding the unforeseen, sailing beyond one's past limitations. Richard laughs at the Madison Avenue talk and the Disneyland imagery. He'd rather focus on ritual dismemberment, with President Bush torn apart like a solar king on a tropical pyramid, arms and legs ripped off and devoured by amazons in strobe light, all the noise in the world pouring out of his mouth, an ocean of garbage, Columbus drifting between dead whales and porpoises near Cuba.

It's New Year's Day, 1493. The smell of death is oppressive, and Columbus can't clear his head. He decides to confess, to reveal his big secret, to finally tell Pinzón the truth about how he planned his voyage. In 1489, he says, a ship sailing north from the Gold Coast got caught in a savage east wind, got blown toward Puerto Rico, at that time completely unknown, got shattered there on the rocks, but most of the crew were quickly rescued, given food by the very same Taino tribe that's now getting royally screwed. Soon they tried to set sail for Spain, but they ran out of food. Only three survived, washing up on the Azores, where Columbus worked making maps at the time. Two of them soon died, but the third, the Captain, lived for maybe three weeks, giving Columbus crucial information. Columbus quickly worked up elaborate maps that he showed to the Queen, who thought they were nice, but had strong words for Columbus about his future, claiming that three main steps can be seen in response to a great innovation: first, people doubt its existence; then, they deny its importance; finally they give the credit to someone else, and you're left there defenseless—a feeling that Charlotte knows only too well when her body grows tense with invasion.

Charlotte's not convinced that it's really Jim Morrison inside her. The guy in her group might just be picking up that her husband's a rock star. But when the Columbus persona begins to take over, she feels that she might be Morrison again. Her confusion grows, branching toward a red butterfly smashed on a windshield, a 1960 pontiac used in a movie about Neil Diamond, a book about cannibals getting trashed in *The Washington Post*, a fake milkman, a floppy disk in a litterbox, three dead cats in a pinball parlor, a massive oak tree throwing tranquil shade on a murderer's birthplace, an amazing map of a country that doesn't exist anymore, a fake nightmare, a bald man sweeping up under a broken-down bridge because he lives there, Columbus confessing his fear of not impressing the Queen or his mother.

Columbus laughs and Pinzón laughs. The Admiral's fear sounds funny. It's got the form of a bird crashing into a bridge in late summer twilight, or a bowling alley snack bar getting bombed, and Pinzón gets an idea: let Señor Columbus waste his youth pursuing vain obsessions. Pinzón wants to get back to Spain, take credit for finding the Indies, show off some of the Taino gold he's collected, and show off the Tainos too, getting a really great price from the local circuses or the marketplace.

The men of the *Niña* get restless feeling victimized and put upon. Why do they have to keep drifting around giving names to dumb little islands, seeming to look for the Great Khan but secretly searching for amazons? On the voyage across he often said, "We'll get there when we get there!" But now he's not sure what to say. He knows true sailing is dead. North doesn't seem to be where it was, so now his compass won't function. A massive calm sets in. The trade winds drop. The sea is a huge bronze gong, vibrating light in the long afternoons, and pressure builds. The crew's eardrums pop. The sky comes down like a dark-feathered bird with a bloody beak, fierce talons.

Columbus knows that time can't really go backwards, that an informational barrier separates what he does now from the past, a barrier of things taking place in one particular sequence. There's almost no chance at all of all those billions of things taking place in reverse, occurring in the very same order, and under precisely the same conditions, and thus even though in theory time could move back into the past, the likelihood that it will is infinitesimal. If even one small thing took place out of sequence, Columbus might end up in a different past, and this of course would have a profound effect on who and where he is now. So Columbus decides to call his crew together and make a pronouncement: Space by itself and time by itself are doomed to fade away. Only space and time combined will preserve any full sense of being!

The men try to nod in response, though some of them snicker and elbow each other's ribs. Later among themselves they begin to feel that the Admiral's losing it. It's clear to them that if life began with random chemical changes, it would have taken a vast amount of time to reach its current state, the almost inconceivably complex relations we find in nature today. In fact, these chemical changes would have had to begin perhaps ten billion years before the beginning of time. For most of the crew this thought is pure insanity. Most of them agree that it's time for mutiny.

The Admiral's informers warn him just in time. He appears on deck. He admits that what he said before might have been rash. He claims that we can know the world only because we share its condition, because it works through the same process, the same motions and relations, that once created and now continue to govern human life. A murmur spreads on deck. This proclamation is more to their liking, and those who don't agree at least admit that it's worth debating. The Admiral's informers tell him privately that he's in good shape, that the crew's impressed with the fact that he can live in contradictions, that even if his thinking is based on dialectical motions, it's not merely based on the play of crude oppositions.

Richard gets the idea of taking footage from a Columbus movie, Hollywood black and white scenes of the Admiral braving waves in a savage night, cutting it up, splicing in cartoons of Noah's Ark, adding in strange dialogue, throwing in canned laughter at all the wrong moments, filling up the sea with uncooked hot dogs, burnt pancakes, maybe a few brief scenes from the recent San Francisco earthquake. Bob could appear on stage dressed up as the president, maps of Latin American countries painted on each of his drums, behind him footage of southern Iraq in flames, oil on the Persian Gulf, then Bosch's *Garden of Delights*, a close-up of the painting showing a pig with a big black hat and a wicked smile, a knife between two ears, and Richard leaves the studio feeling elated.

When he and Bob get home Dan Quayle's on TV making a speech, explaining why it's crucial to spend a billion dollars each day on weapons research. He says he needs to begin by clearly stating his basic assumptions, his belief that all connections between the world and our means of describing it—connections between reality and representational systems—are unknowable, that what reality is in itself is unknowable, that the only way to approach it is to prove that former methods of describing the world were self-deceived, to eliminate through careful critique those deeply ingrained beliefs that clearly falsify the perceivable world, that no explanation can even begin to account for the simplest process, but can only hope to simulate its form, providing a model but not a real description, and certainly not a prescription—but Richard's no longer tuned in.

His thoughts are drifting back to Columbus telling himself that the world's not flat, then appearing on deck to make sure the crew's not expecting to sail off the edge. None of them think they really will, but Columbus preaches as if they were all in the grip of primal terrors, giving himself a chance to enjoy his own eloquence. He and his men get so caught up in his voice they forget to keep track of the ship. They sail off the edge of the world without even knowing it, an act made more complex by the fact that it's not the edge of space they've sailed across but the edge of time, an edge beyond which Columbus becomes an information system, a massive range of motions without visible dimensions, a shark with a calculating machine stitched into the place of its genitals, a sequence of numbers that only repeats after more than a million digits, an algorithmic dance that appears on screen like a Chinese carpet, the smallest detail of which contains an image of the entire design, fading into the gloom of a Gothic twilight, a series of murders that never took place, an unfamiliar face in bed, a sequence of strangely connected events that ends and begins with a missing head, a psycho-linguistics major getting seduced by a sexy beer ad, a general making a televised victory speech getting stuck between syllables, a doctor's patients finally figuring out that they only seem to be cured, the future dissolving into a long-discredited Renaissance theory, a person walking away from a pointless apology, a person losing his fiancée because he makes too much noise—all punched up on a glowing digital screen, getting smashed by an ex-defensive tackle's foot in a fist fight, an office quarrel that breaks out on the 29th floor and quickly spreads, quite soon taking over three floors of the Gulf & Western Building, the glass of which reflects a morning sky where clouds are mirrors, drifting over the sea as Columbus comes to the end of his eloquent speech, then feels completely fatigued and quietly disappears into his cabin, muttering that Beatriz de Peraza gave him a workout, and he badly needs to sleep. He's there for weeks. It's almost embarrassing. Although his men can certainly sympathize with his exhaustion, his need to sleep after so many torrid nights with Ms. de Peraza, they nonetheless feel the need for inspiration, for an image of Columbus pacing the deck, a vigilant captain. Soon they erect an icon made of painted wood and chiseled stone, Columbus peering into the night, unbending in his devotion—leading Richard back to the screen, where the nation's young vice-president reaches a critical point in his argument.

His central example is based on communications, on the fact that the present limit on silicon technology is a function of the speed with which electrons move through a semiconductor. He pauses to let the point sink in, gazing out from the picture tube with a firm and somber expression. He then admits that words like *silicon* and *electron*, no matter how scientific they sound, are nothing more than representations, verbal images of non-verbal entities. Consider, for example, how the words would change if the first atomic theories had been developed on the basis of waves instead of particles. Then our focus would not have been on silicon or electrons, but on indices of resistance, on patterns of refraction, and again the vice-president pauses, letting the language grow in the minds of his audience. Soon there's applause, faint at first but spreading, building in volume, shaking TV screens all over the nation, shattering picture tubes, dripping out like jelly into clean suburban parlors, filling living rooms coast to coast with vague disturbing pleasure.

When Columbus wakes, he feels like he might be three very different people, talking in turn but not to each other. They're speaking towards others who aren't really there, and apparently don't need to be, or anyway not completely, a complication that makes what Columbus once thought of himself seem obsolete, a feeling that's like getting drunk one night and smashing your daughter's fishbowl. After all, the Admiral wants to make sense when he talks to himself, and he also wants a good listener when he talks to himself. He can't find one. Everyone in the Admiral's mind seems utterly unconcerned. They're caught in things that can't be defined. They're lost in representations. When Columbus talks to himself there's no one listening. He feels unable to focus on what he ought to do next. It gets out of hand. Columbus lives in the constant fear of losing control. He can't shake it.

Jimmy knows that Richard wants this constant fear in the video. But he's also aware that it can't be translated well into video images. Unless it's done in a really extreme theatrical way it won't come across, and he knows that Richard wants the Admiral's fear to be secret and subtle. Richard tries to look paranoid in the video, and Bob tries to look both blank and scared as he pounds on his drums without keeping a beat. But unless things are done in a blatant way, they don't look right on camera, which means that a telegenic emotion looks like a face in a coloring book, lacking the careful shadings of feelings that people would rather conceal, or feelings that they aren't even fully aware of. Jimmy decides that it's better to try it without the paranoid posturing, that Richard needs to look assured and sexy for the camera. It's what Richard really does best, even if it's not right for the lyrics.

The subway scene gets cut, and in its place, there's footage of Custer, or rather footage of Errol Flynn from the movie "They Died With Their Boots On." There's also altered footage of Buffalo Bill from a fifties TV show, slaughtering hundreds of buffalo each day for fun and profit, juxtaposed with woodcuts of the Tainos getting burned alive, spliced with shots of Bob really bashing his drums and looking angry. A shot of Bob's face then becomes George Bush on the tube addressing the nation, looking sad but firm declaring war on a country smaller than Texas, cutting back to Richard as Columbus gazing into the dark, a dim light in the distance, burning oil in the Persian Gulf.

Columbus gets rid of a waterspout by reading *Revelations*, raising a sword to the sky, moving it over his head in a circle, carving into the clouds what might be described as a copyright sign. Suddenly, as the storm dissolves, he's faced with the island of amazons, women with powerful bodies on the shore waving flowers of welcome. Hojeda thinks it's got to be a trick, but Columbus gets pulled in. He wants to make love with the Queen, who's acting seductive. Soon she's got Columbus in a hammerlock, and he can't get free. Most of his men get knocked out cold on the beach in hand-to-hand combat. They're simply no match for the amazons, who put them and their admiral back on the ship, tied up unconscious, letting a very strong series of trade winds blow them back out to sea.

The *Niña* drifts in the trades for days, Columbus in a semi-conscious state stretched out on the poop deck, haunted by delirious thoughts, talk of a "radical remedy," men and women wrestling on a stage in a club called The Gold Mine—until Hojeda wakes him up with a bucket of ice-cold water.

When Columbus gets back to the site of the wreck of his flagship, the Taino king, Canabo, tells him Pinzón's on his way back to Spain. Columbus feels confused at first, but then it all makes perfect sense: Pinzón wants to get back first and claim to have found Cathay and the Indies, telling the Queen that the Admiral would have turned back a day before landfall, having lost his nerve, so totally spooked he thought he'd seen mermaids. But he, Pinzón, was able to keep the goals of the voyage in mind, resisting the weird obsessions Columbus fell victim to in the tropics. Columbus gets mad imagining Pinzón playing up to the Queen, sounding really persuasive, showing off Taino slaves and gold dust, becoming a future household word, Admiral of the Ocean Sea, reaping all the financial rewards that really belong to Columbus. Canabo says Pinzón left two days before, so he's got a good head start. It's all Columbus can do to keep from tearing out his own eyeballs.

Pinzón's gotten popular with his crew because of his big tattoo. He claims he got it from people who knew the descendants of Marco Polo, who'd been to Cathay and learned the art of tattooing from court prostitutes, who claimed they'd learned the art from a place to the south, later called Polynesia. Columbus always thought the story was nonsense, an obvious fabrication Pinzón used to get attention, a way to make it seem that he already knew Cathay and the Indies, that he already had connections with what Columbus was trying to find. Nonetheless, the tattoo has always caught the crew's attention. They like the fact that the future's been sketched out on the first mate's chest, a sequence of numbers that only repeats after more than a million digits, an algorithmic dance on a strangely glowing screen, a huge carpet. The future's right there to see, except that the men have no frame of reference. To them, a CRT looks like some weird cabalistic symbol, meaning it's got to be carefully studied. And Pinzón won't be studied, won't turn himself into a book, won't stop while the men read his chest, so they get only glimpses—fragments that mess with the way they normally think and keep them guessing, a little game to play when his demands become depressing. They know that X need not equal X all the time, but at least it *sounds* like it does, and in their situation even a possible truth is music. It keeps them entertained, puts a human face on chaos, and they work for Pinzón with more gusto than they ever displayed for Columbus.

Columbus growls at the waves and the waves growl back. The clouds grow distant. He draws a pentagram on the deck, begins a conjuration. He calls the name Pinzón and the name of the devil, mixing the words with Arabian alchemical incantations. Soon Pinzón himself appears, rising out of the diagram in smoke and borrowed thunder. But he's also at this moment still on the *Pinta*, two hundred miles northeast, having a dream about changing his course, and when he wakes the dream controls what he thinks and does. He sets a new course, aiming right into a storm that nearly destroys him.

Columbus takes off into the deep, blessed with strong and following winds, and soon they reach a speed no ship has ever known before. Infinite space each way they look, the men of Columbus begin to relax, mesmerized by the gleaming rise and fall of the waves all around them, nursing the wounds they received on the island of amazons. But soon the winds die down. Huge clouds gather in the north. The sea turns cold and the waves refuse to keep following. There's nothing behind the ship now but folded cardboard. Warm air moving north runs into cold air moving south. The poles conspire, producing impossible crossing winds and crossing seas, pushing Columbus in several directions at once. Waves taller than the Great Pyramids pitch up in front of the ship, drop on the deck like bursting boxes of paper clips. Columbus begins to think he'll die face-down on a broken mirror, but finally they reach the island of Santa Maria, in the Azores, anchoring near a small town where they find a sheepish Pinzón and the *Pinta*, driven on shore by the same storm two days before. Columbus meets Pinzón in the town square looking for food and supplies for the ship, and both try to look like nothing's wrong. They talk about the weather. A weirdly concealed sense of anger spreads through the town and soon takes tangible form. The shores grow dim with a highly theatrical sense of impending doom. There's darkness in all the windows, even though it's light outside, and the white stone walls of the houses crack and seem on the verge of collapsing.

It's precisely this feeling that comes over Charlotte at times when she can't sleep at night, waking up with Columbus behind her face and in her body. But the group she's been going to seems to be helping her find better ways of assuming control, giving her host personality more centrality. She starts to think that maybe she'll soon be close to a normal existence—until one night, in a bar, things get pretty grim again. She's there to meet a friend who's been delayed, so she sits at the bar for a drink. The TV set shows M-TV non-stop around the clock, but most of the time the sound's turned off and people play songs in the juke-box. What's on the screen doesn't match what people hear, though at times they can't really tell, especially after they've had a few or get caught up in talking. On screen right now, though Charlotte at first doesn't notice, is one of Richard's earlier videos, focused on masochistic sex. And while she's waiting five guys try to pick her up, four of them idiots. But there's one she wants to like. He's really cute. He reminds her of Richard, although she doesn't make the connection at first—not until she sees Richard moving his ass on the TV screen, and catching sight of him breaks the spell. She suddenly thinks the new guy's really dull. But if the sound had been turned on, things might have seemed quite different. She would have remembered that Richard's words were always like his actions, that his songs were filled with self-destructive rage and pointless violence. But the images on the TV screen remain silent. She only sees how good Richard looks on stage. She thinks of his body in bed. Feelings come back that she thought were dead. Out to sea again, she's Columbus.

Columbus keeps his courage not by imagining future power and fame, but by thinking of how much pleasure he'll get from knowing those who doubted him were dead wrong. His only question is whether he'll have more fun being openly scornful, or whether it's better to keep it inside and just be secretly satisfied. Of course, had the first mate gotten home first, Columbus would have had no choice. Whatever satisfaction he'd felt would need to remain a secret, a quiet pleasure that soon would no doubt be destroyed by bitterness, or by the penniless state that he'd soon be reduced to. So as he chats with Pinzón, there's a lot on his mind—or rather, a lot on *part* of his mind. The rest of his mind feels nothing. It's like a phone call put on hold, where callers are forced to sit passively while muzak plays, or top-forty, and a voice comes briefly back, please hold, more muzak, then a quick voice again, and soon there's not a whole lot on anyone's mind, not even on part of it.

The feeling that the world's on hold gives Richard acute anxiety. He thinks about how Pinzón will soon commit suicide, arriving home to find that the claim he's sent ahead has been ignored, that Queen Isabella refuses to talk with anyone but Columbus. Richard would like to make Pinzón out to be a tragic figure, like Judas or Brutus or maybe Columbus himself a mere ten years later, having lost all the titles and honors promised him by the Queen, dying in poverty knowing how much of a mess he'd made in the Indies.

But as he leaves the studio Richard's thoughts get crushed by New York noise, garbage trucks and sirens, motorcycles, endless honking horns, all of which make Richard think that the modern world is a huge mistake, that everything's been downhill since 1800, that everything's been downhill since 1492—and why stop there: everything's been downhill since 10,000 years before the birth of Christ, when agriculture began to appear and develop all over the world, and complicated social organization became unavoidable. It's just a small jump, he thinks, from horse and plow to horn and siren, and he plans to make his next video about noise and the death of intelligence, even though it's occurred to him that the music he makes is a form of noise, that what's called popular culture feeds the noise that makes thought impossible. He wants to play on this irony in the video he's planning, but he knows he'll have to do it in such a way that the music makes money, appealing to those who've come to accept noise pollution and don't mind consuming it.

He thinks of Charlotte, thinks of their final blow-out nearly five months ago. The argument that led to the violence began around this topic. Richard got mad when Charlotte ridiculed his attack on technology, when she told him the world had been vastly improved by the changes Richard was trashing, that to say it all ought to be destroyed because it made things noisy was absurd, that people would never get rid of noise if it meant getting rid of convenience.

These words had made Richard crazy, even though he could see in a way what she meant. To be sure, the pre-technological world had been rough, in no sense a paradise. If it had been, no one would have been willing to change. And besides, there was no turning back. Even as the world came closer and closer to drowning in garbage, very few people did anything to prevent it, even if they said they were deeply concerned. And in his more honest moments, he could see that he was one of them, that the statements he made with his music weren't really actions against the machine—indeed, they relied on technology for their final manifestations. But the rage he felt when faced with the pointless noise of midtown traffic, thousands honking their horns in sheer frustration, had long since pushed him past the point of listening to reason, especially when there was more to Charlotte's ridicule than reason—it gave her the chance to ventilate her own unspoken frustrations, to push things to a point where a physical fight was much more than likely.

Columbus knows that fighting isn't the best way to get what he wants. He knows that he's got a better chance with Pinzón if he just pretends to be nice, nodding along with all the lies the man tells him. Pinzón feels like a monkey swallowing ball-point pens, like a false coat of arms, like a word around which other words change their significance.

The sun goes down behind Pinzón's head, and the landscape suddenly seems to be arranged around his face. Columbus reaches into the first mate's head and pulls his brain out, parts the flesh and bone in Pinzón's chest and spreads it wide, putting his brain inside while yanking his heart out, closing his chest with his right hand and putting his heart in his head with his left.

Pinzón grins with all his teeth. The sunset colors deepen. Pinzón grips the Admiral's head and twists it maybe ten full turns, holding it in place for a second or two, then letting it go. It spins back around really quickly, making a noise like an outboard motor, the Admiral's nose and teeth and eyes becoming blurred with motion. His long blond hair makes a whistling sound, cutting its way through the cool of the day. Sweat flies off his head in all directions. He grins back at Pinzón with all his teeth and the colors deepen. The two men embrace, and one thing now seems absolutely clear: that any system of representation is nothing more than a model, a rigid spatial construct, but may nonetheless have a crucial effect on how we perceive the far more complex world that the system is modeling. The fluid shape of space and time begins to seem quite static, like statues of people cheering at baseball games in the centerfield bleachers. The conquest of nature can't be delayed any longer. It's like a really mean guy in the shadows just around the corner, smiling with all his teeth and waiting to stuff a pie in a grandmother's face, or like mathematical diagrams on drafting boards in smoky rooms, where very smart young men drink instant coffee.

Columbus tends to think that the world is a diagram of perspective, that anything that won't fit into that diagram is defective. He's trained to perceive the world as if it extended out from his eyes, as if it were some kind of logical arrangement focused on him, as if it all funneled in toward a point about half an inch behind his face, as if his thoughts were not already shaping and timing physical space, regulating its motions, making them turn in measured circles, making animals seem as if they were born to live in the circus. His mind is Ptolemy's map, a careful grid of calculations, claiming to be completely free of moods and expectations, a formal ensemble of abstract arcs and planes on flat white pages, as if the Christian mission were somehow coterminous with rational space, as if the world were a Eurocaucasian pig pen, or a table set for a group of wealthy white men.

When Columbus gets back, he decides to win the Queen's heart with lavish descriptions, making repeated reference to the sea with its clear blue depth, its emerald waves and sparkling crests and its huge and mild opalescence, the rugged coastlines bordered by murmuring surf, lush green mountains, flowering trees of a marvelous brilliance unlike any in Europe. But the travel book adjectives don't have much effect. The Queen's not impressed. Her only concern is the Great Khan, or how much gold these islands that lead to Cathay might some day produce. Columbus doesn't have much gold, but he does have human specimens, fifteen slaves that impress the Queen greatly, even though ten of them quickly die. She sees there's a lot of potential, tells Columbus to make a new voyage, bringing back new slaves or gold, or both—and he'd better bring both.

Columbus feels like a skinhead in a bowling league. He's dead with fatigue, and Richard knows that what he wants to say can't go much further. Jimmy's already ambivalent about all the ambivalent images. His job might be in jeopardy if the video's not a big success, and it might not be. The nation doesn't want people trashing its fantasies. Why force a population that's already badly confused and deeply in debt—a population drugged on false information, stale amusements—to see that their world was formed in the wake of a genocide, that the Tainos would have been smart if they'd found a way to kill Columbus, to poison all his men or sink their ships or give them diseases. But Jimmy's quick to point out that more would have come. It was just a matter of time. The Age of Exploration was already underway, and the stage was set. The Christian Eurocaucasian machine was in place and ready for action.

Words like these make Richard feel depressed. They remind him of Charlotte, the kind of acrid logic she would use to shoot down his ideas. It's not that Richard can't stand any critique, but more that he gets pissed off when people show contempt, make him feel like a jerk. Critique is fine when it shows respect and leads him to make his music and his videos more complex. But Richard knows that even his own critiques aren't always respectful, that oversimplistic opinions tend to make him feel contempt. Indeed, contempt is what he feels about the impending celebrations, the crowds going crazy worshiping an idol they don't understand, and aren't about to take the time to learn about.

He thinks of Columbus stepping on shore in San Salvador for the first time. A gull banks down and shits on his head, and the crew breaks out in laughter, which the Tainos interpret as pain. They offer gifts in consolation, and soon they're breaking their backs in gold mines, killing themselves in despair. Richard thinks he wants cocaine. He wants to go to Bermuda. He wants to go out and buy cassettes of himself on stage in Cuba, belting out a song about the need for perestroika, claiming that it had nothing to do with Wall Street or Madison Avenue. But Fidel wanted nothing to do with him, a white boy mouthing grad school poli-sci platitudes, getting rich on images of a Hollywood-style revolution, voguing around on stage instead of sleeping with a machine gun.

At times, Richard's fully aware of the contradictions, but since he's not prepared to take steps to change his situation, he's trapped in the self-contempt that's always right behind his public face, a feeling he's grown so accustomed to that he's often not even aware of it. At times, however, the feelings emerge. He moves his right hand up to his mouth and reaches in as far as he can, past his teeth and down his throat and into a place where he's not obsolete, where neck-ties have all turned upside-down to become exclamation points, where not all passion seems completely self-deceived or pointless, where darkness turns into light when the temperature drops more than eighteen degrees, where Charlotte's body building seems to be more than mere self-objectification, where mirrors don't poison his blood by turning it into medication. But the trouble is that sometimes Richard's hand won't come back out, at least not right away, and it gets embarrassing if he's in a crowd, so most of the time he can't really do much more than sit with his feelings, try to explain them in crude psychological terms he no longer believes in, and it's at this point that sado-masochistic desires begin, slowly forming an arc becoming a snake that's eating its tail, but not quite a copyright sign or the smile of a nation drunk on junkmail, leaving Richard space to put his feelings into music.

Bob's made up to look just like George Bush on drums in the White House. The Oval Office windows have all been shattered. The view outside leaks in at times, but most of the time it stays where it is, fading into fires on the Persian Gulf, then fires in Jamaica, Spanish boats and guns offshore, Tainos dead from exhaustion. The drums are made from human skulls, a savage beat propping up what Richard sings, vocal distortion, blending with a contorted fuzz guitar pattern, computerized amplification, words like arms getting torn from their sockets, dimes in a beggar's pockets, like a photograph magnified so many times that a tenement looks like a brain cell, that the President's tie clip starts to look like Dante trapped on the rivers of hell, that the left thigh of the Columbus Circle statue looks like buffalo meat, or like a surgeon trapped in a magic spell, or like a dead clown's feet, that an exclamation point begins to look like a mushroom cloud, or like a disguised presentation of something that's not for the most part allowed, that might be better left unsaid, and has been. And at this point the lyrics change: images of paradise, Columbus on his third voyage near the coast of Venezuela, using his astrolabe to decide that the world isn't round, but shaped like a pear, with a part that bulges out like a female breast, and its nipple is paradise, closer to the sky than the rest of the world. But there's no third voyage.

NEW WORLD ORDER

Jimmy's recently read that Columbus died before he could sail again, that all the subsequent voyages were supervised by imposters, so the paradise image gets dropped, replaced by a holographic backdrop, a 3-D *Santa María* going down off Cape Haitien, Bob as President Bush doing steel drum riffs in a White House garden.

Bob and Richard agree with Jimmy that things are getting much tighter. But the night's not quite complete. There's no cocaine. They've all got the craving. Richard finally breaks down and says he'll go outside to find some. He knows just where to go. He takes a long walk. The night feels perfect, as if what he was looking for was anything but addiction, was something which became more intense but less defined the closer he came, was nothing like a new world made suddenly visible through morning mist, indeed was more like a world that was doing fine by itself, didn't need to be found, didn't need to become a stomping ground for a stale and self-deceived culture.

On East 29th he goes past an open window. Glancing inside, he sees a nude man jerking off in a big black chair, eyes intent on his TV set, a frantic announcer's voice invading the room, describing what sounds to Richard like a wrestling match between women. But when he stops at a bar on the corner, he sees the same match on the TV screen, a really powerful woman throwing a man all over the ring. At first, he can't believe his eyes. But it's true. It's really Charlotte. She's calling herself Beatrice McCoy, and the TV announcer calls her "The Real McCoy" when she slams the man down on the mat, pushing his face down wrenching his arm in a hammerlock, causing him to moan with pain and pound the mat and finally concede. Richard's really turned on. But only at first, and then he feels crazy, just what he felt the night she won the Ms. Olympia contest. He doesn't like the attention she's getting. It makes him feel insecure. Even though he tells himself that TV wrestling is nonsense, mere theatrical farce, he can't get beyond the feeling of jealousy. So instead of calling it by its true name, he goes back out with a beer in a bag to buy cocaine down on Avenue C, hoping to lose himself in the madding crowd, but the city seems empty. Despite the fact that a TV's on in every window he passes, urban living rooms filled with the mythic pulse of pale blue light, no one seems to be left alive to see what's on the screen. The voices jabbing out onto the street from the rooms all seem electronic, trapped in highly affected scripted speech, convulsive pacing. It makes perfect sense, Richard thinks, that the city's caught in its own huge absence, that it's come to the point where the TV requires no audience. Suddenly all the sets click off on their own at once—dead silence. The noise only clicks back on more than ten hours later.

Meanwhile Charlotte's ecstatic: ten overwhelming victories in a row, ten top contenders! Now she can challenge the men's world heavyweight champion. It was only after Richard left that she'd followed up on an offer, becoming Bea McCoy and wrestling twice a month for good money. Of course, it wasn't really the money she wanted, but the feeling she'd always had with Richard in winning their physical fights, a thrill that in the past had always been mixed with strong contempt—for him, to be sure, but also herself. The whole thing was so idiotic. But now she can get that thrill without contempt. It's really amazing. And the man jerking off on 29th Street agrees. He's in seventh heaven.

Charlotte goes to sleep with "Goodbye Columbus" on the stereo, but wakes to a loud announcer's voice on her digital clock radio, to Richard's voice on her phone machine, to car alarms and sirens, garbage trucks and public busses, the sound of a morning talk show coming down from the condo above her. She's trapped in a jail of noise, and it's only been light outside for an hour. She wears her walkman headset into the shower.

She plays back Richard's message—something about her new profession. She hears him say the name Bea McCoy several times, and she hears the words bitch and cunt, then something about Martinino Bay, an island of radical remedies. But he's all coked out and the words run together. She's glad she's got a phone machine to protect her. So now the truth is out. He knows that she's living out their shared fantasy, doing precisely what he'd always tried to imagine her doing, a masturbation fantasy that at first he'd felt quite perverse about, but which now went quite well with what she planned to do herself, as if she were some kind of modern Athena, hatching herself from the mind of a tyrant god—or media demigod.

Later that morning Charlotte's agent calls with a message for Bea McCoy: she's got a match next month with number one, the male wrestling champion. The Columbia Broadcasting System is already planning a nationwide special. She's really sure she can win. She feels all day like she's in seventh heaven. And she feels like she's finally got

NEW WORLD ORDER

the strength to pursue an old ambition, to put her thoughts into words—she's already got her first essay planned, a quincentenial article proving Columbus was really a woman, that the second voyage got cancelled because men couldn't accept her achievements. She doesn't have any evidence—she's not even sure that the second voyage got cancelled—but the feeling inside is really strong. Somehow she knows it's true, and she's eager to start doing careful research. But resting in bed that night making notes in her journal she feels her mind slipping, or rather, beginning to take the familiar shape of her disorder. She starts to feel that the words aren't hers. She can't control their direction. She knows that the sound of a word and the sense of a word aren't at all the same thing. But it suddenly seems clear that the sense of the word isn't what the word is in itself, that both the sound and sense of the word are separate from the world of things, and she can't seem to find the world of things right now. She's trapped in language. She tells herself she's out to sea, and it's true. Again, she's Columbus.

Walking down the streets of Palos, everywhere hailed as a hero, Columbus stops at Prince Henry the Masturbator's luxury townhouse. Prince Henry had been instrumental in launching the Age of Exploration, working with state-of-the-art navigational tools and outrageous insights, and Columbus feels he'll get his ego stroked if he stops for a brief morning chat. After all, he's taken Prince Henry's ideas and given them credence, proving beyond all doubt what before had only been wild speculation.

But when he meets the Masturbator's gaze from his big black armchair, their eyes exchange a savage understanding, that the world will never be the same again, and it never was, that the Indies will one day become a region of busboys, that numbers will never be anything more than a well-defined collection of mostly indefinable objects, that a letter from the Pope is like waking up with a six-foot hot dog, or stealing someone's dog to win a bet, or bouncing a check on your boss, or painting mirrors black in a posh motel room, or like a map of Maine burning up in a brothel in Alberta, a thousand dolphins getting killed by tuna companies daily, a roach in Rome, a game show emcee losing his mind on LSD, a glass eye factory getting destroyed by an earthquake. The Masturbator's gaze gets more intense with every second, and Columbus can't look away. It's clear that space can be replaced, that nothing is indispensable, that everything has a price, that

Copernicus might be right, that God plays dice, that grammar changes words in the same way time transforms the world, that laughter serves to cover certain things up, revealing others, that the pain on the Masturbator's face can't be explained in rational terms, that he feels like his mind is a can of worms, a place that hungry birds might like, that Columbus needs a finger to plug the dike of his guilty ambition, that all the maps in the world are filled with distortions, that when the sun comes up there's a little black dot in the west, a cold fire in the south, a really tense feeling in everyone's mouth, a box of teeth in the desert. The moment throbs. It grows. It can't be stopped. It's multiplied by ten. It's clear that neither man will ever move again—dead silence.

ABOUT THE AUTHOR

STEPHEN-PAUL MARTIN is the co-editor of *Central Park* magazine in New York City. He is the author of twelve collections of fiction, poetry, criticism and visual writing. He currently lives with his wife Peg in Brooklyn.